Mike switched off the engine and pulled off his helmet. He turned to her, his astonishingly handsome face flushed and happy. "Wasn't that great?" he asked. "I could ride like that forever."

Just looking at him was enough to make Jessica's heart ache.

"It was," she agreed, her smile reflecting his enthusiasm. "It was totally fantastic."

Mike climbed down, and then, before Jessica could follow, he lifted her off and into his arms.

"What are you doing?" she yelled, laughing. "Put me down!"

"Never," Mike answered, his golden eyes suddenly serious. "This is my idea of heaven. My bike, an open road, and the most wonderful girl in the world snuggled up against me. I'll never let you go, Jess. Not ever."

Jessica wrapped her arms around his neck, overwhelmed with love. "You couldn't get rid of me if you tried," she said softly. "I'm never leaving you."

"Really, Jess?" His stare was so intent, she almost felt that he was looking into her soul. "Do you really mean that? You'll stay with me forever?"

She leaned her forehead to his. "You know I mean it," she answered. "I've never meant anything more."

"Then prove it," Mike said, his voice a whisper. "Marry me. We'll ride out to Las Vegas. Marry me now."

SWEET VALLEY UNIVERSITY ™

Anything for Love

Written by
Laurie John

Created by
FRANCINE PASCAL

BANTAM BOOKS
NEW YORK • TORONTO • LONDON • SYDNEY • AUCKLAND

RL 6, age 12 and up

ANYTHING FOR LOVE
A Bantam Book / April 1994

Sweet Valley High® *and Sweet Valley University*™
are trademarks of Francine Pascal
Conceived by Francine Pascal
Produced by Daniel Weiss Associates, Inc.
33 West 17th Street
New York, NY 10011

ISBN: 0-553-56311-4

Published simultaneously in the United States and Canada

Bantam Books are published by Bantam Books, a division of Bantam
Doubleday Dell Publishing Group, Inc. Its trademark, consisting of the
words "Bantam Books" and the portrayal of a rooster, is Registered in
U.S. Patent and Trademark Office and in other countries. Marca
Registrada. Bantam Books, 1540 Broadway, New York, New York 10036.

PRINTED IN THE UNITED STATES OF AMERICA

OPM   0 9 8 7 6 5 4 3

For John Stewart Carmen

Chapter One

Jessica Wakefield's long golden hair streamed behind her in the wind as the big motorcycle sped along and the landscape passed in a blur of blue and green. She caught her breath as the lowrider took another sharp turn. Riding down the coast with Mike McAllery was unlike anything she'd done before. Most people Jessica knew took this road because it was high in the hills and had a spectacular view of the beach and the ocean below. Mike took this road because it was narrow, steep, and winding and he could put his customized bike through its paces. Most people Jessica knew enjoyed listening to music and talking as they drove, but Mike enjoyed the rumble of the motorcycle's 1000-cc engine and the sharp thrust of the wind.

The bike leaned left and Jessica, her arms around Mike, leaned with it.

I love it, too, she told herself. *I love the excitement and the danger, I love feeling the wind in my face. . . .* Her thoughts broke off while she spat out something the wind had blown into her mouth. *I don't even mind getting bugs in my hair,* she continued, refusing to think about what might have been in her mouth, or how tangled her hair would be by the time the ride was over. Jessica tightened her hold on the hard, leather-clad body in front of her. *More than anything, though, I love Mike. I want anything he wants. I'll do anything he does.*

Jessica closed her eyes as the bike pulled out to overtake an eighteen-wheeler. When she heard Mike's whoop of triumph at having passed the enormous truck and felt the bike pull back into its lane, she opened her eyes again.

Although she didn't like to admit it even to herself, Mike did things Jessica didn't really approve of. Like take too many chances. And there were other, more important things, too—things that hurt and confused her. As loving and caring as Mike was, he was also possessive and demanding. If Jessica wanted to do something on her own in the evening, he got angry and jealous. He couldn't seem to understand why she'd want to spend time with anyone else when she could be with him. As far as Mike was concerned, even her college classes weren't that important—he expected her to cut them whenever he wanted her to. "You're my baby now," he'd say. "Don't you want to be with me?"

If she risked his anger and went somewhere without him or even if she was more than a few minutes late getting home, he'd storm out of their apartment and spend the night in one of his favorite bars, doing things Jessica was afraid to imagine.

Jessica's sea-green eyes clouded as she remembered the nights she'd cried herself to sleep since moving in with Mike a little over a month ago. And the mornings she'd woken up to find him passed out on the sofa, smelling of beer, cigarette smoke, and some other woman's perfume. Jessica blinked back a tear that hadn't been caused by the wind. She didn't like to think about Mike and other women.

The bike picked up speed as they hurtled downhill, the engine whining and the wind shricking. Mike had sworn that he would never cheat on her, that she was the only woman he had ever really loved, but Jessica knew how attractive he was to women—and how attractive they were to him. In her heart, Jessica was sure that Mike didn't really want anyone else. But if she wasn't there to tell him that she loved him, he started having doubts, and then he started looking around for a pretty woman to cheer him up.

Jessica pressed herself against Mike's strong, lean back. There was never any shortage of pretty women willing to cheer up Michael McAllery, that was one thing Jessica knew for sure. Hadn't she even seen one or two of them with him? He always had a good excuse—excuses Jessica believed—but she couldn't completely deny all the stories she'd heard about him. She couldn't completely forget the way he looked at those women—or the way they looked back.

Jessica came out of her reverie as the bike turned off the road and into the parking lot of a shabby-looking diner. She'd been so lost in her worries about Mike that she hadn't even realized they were slowing down.

Mike switched off the engine and pulled off his helmet. He turned to her, his astonishingly handsome face flushed and happy. "What do you think?" he asked. "Wasn't that great? I could ride like that forever."

Just looking at him was enough to make Jessica's heart ache.

"It was," she agreed, her smile reflecting his enthusiasm. "It was totally fantastic."

Mike climbed down, and then, before Jessica could follow, he lifted her off and into his arms.

"What are you doing?" she yelled, laughing. "Put me down!"

"Never," Mike answered, his golden eyes suddenly serious. "This is my idea of heaven. My bike, an open road, and the most wonderful girl in the world snuggled up against me. I'll never let you go, Jess. Not ever."

Jessica wrapped her arms around his neck, overwhelmed with love. "You couldn't get rid of me if you tried," she said softly. "I'm never leaving you."

"Really, Jess?" His stare was so intent, she almost felt that he was looking into her soul. "Do you really mean that? You'll stay with me forever?"

She leaned her forehead to his. "You know I mean it," she answered. "I've never meant anything more."

"Then prove it," said Mike, his voice a whisper. "Marry me. We'll ride out to Las Vegas. Marry me now."

"I don't get it," said Steven Wakefield from behind the newspaper he was reading. "They have nothing in common and they fight all the time, but she still hasn't left him."

Billie looked up from her book, a slightly bemused expression on her face. "Who are you talking about? Prince Charles and Princess Diana? You're living in the past, Steven. They broke up a while ago."

Steven sighed. "No, Billie, I am not talking about Prince Charles and Princess Diana. I'm talking about Jessica and that creep Mike McAllery." He put down the paper and looked over at his girlfriend. "I was sure it wouldn't last once they moved in together. I mean, I could understand if Elizabeth and Todd moved in together. Elizabeth has always been solid and totally devoted. But Jessica?" He made a face. "Jessica's middle name used to be Good Time. Jessica Good Time Wakefield. Her idea of being serious about a guy was going out with him more than twice." He shook his head. "I was sure once she realized how much fun she was missing not living in the dorm with her friends, she'd dump McAllery like the garbage he is."

Billie gave him a look. It was the look that said that Mike McAllery wasn't garbage, he just wasn't Steven's idea of the perfect boyfriend for his sister. She didn't say anything, though. Steven knew this was because she was tired of saying it.

"Well, you were wrong, weren't you?" Billie answered instead. "Elizabeth and Todd broke up, and Jessica has the permanent relationship."

Steven frowned. The breakup of Elizabeth and her long-standing boyfriend, Todd Wilkins, had surprised him even more than Jessica falling for Mike. In fact, Elizabeth had had a hard time adjusting to college life in every way. That was why Steven still hadn't told her that Jessica had moved in with Mike in the apartment below his. A girl who had always been thin and beautiful and had dozens of friends, who had suddenly become friendless and started gaining weight didn't need any more bad news in her life.

"Not permanent, Billie," Steven said. A slight smile appeared on his face. "In fact, it may turn out to be a lot more temporary than Jessica thinks."

"What does that mean?" Billie asked. "You've changed your mind about telling your parents?"

"No, I still don't want to be a stool pigeon, but they might find out anyway." The smile became a little brighter. "After all, Parents' Weekend is coming up soon. How's she going to handle that? They're bound to discover the truth."

Billie laughed. "This is Jessica Wakefield we're talking about, isn't it? From the stories you've told me about her schemes, I don't think she'll have any trouble keeping your parents in the dark." She smiled mischievously. "And anyway, you might be wrong about your parents' reaction if they did find out. I know this has never occurred to you, but they might actually like Mike McAllery."

"Like him?" Steven had never thought that anything with the name Mike McAllery attached to it would make him laugh, but he'd been wrong. He was nearly choking with laughter at the thought of his parents liking Jessica's boyfriend. "Are you joking? *My* parents like Mike McAllery? My parents are reasonable people, Billie. They're responsible, concerned parents. Mike McAllery's a criminal."

Billie smirked. "He drives a '64 Corvette and rides a motorcycle, Steven. That does not make him a criminal."

"Exactly!" Steven crowed. "He has an expensive car and an expensive bike, so he has money."

"If having money were a crime, half the kids at SVU would be in jail," Billie countered.

"Half the kids at SVU aren't over twenty-one and unemployed."

"But he's not unemployed," argued Billie. "He does things to cars."

Steven waved her words away. "*Doing things to cars* isn't exactly a profession, you know."

"It is for some people."

"But not for this guy, Billie. You know as well as I do that's just a front. Whatever he really does for money, that's not it."

Billie shook her head. "You don't know that, Steven. You have no evidence for that at all."

"I don't need evidence," he answered. "All I have to do is look at him with his tricked-out bike, his leather jacket, and his bad attitude."

Billie glared at him over the top of her book. "You're the one with the bad attitude," she snapped. "You went ballistic the second you knew Mike was going out with Jess. You've never given him a chance."

Steven pictured his father in his neat pinstripe suit meeting Mike McAllery in his black motorcycle gear. "Well, now I am going to give him a chance," said Steven. "I'm going to give him the chance to hang himself."

Elizabeth Wakefield looked up from her notebook as the door opened. The nurse who had shown Elizabeth to this room looked in at her, her expression concerned.

"Is she still asleep?" the nurse whispered.

Elizabeth glanced over at the still figure on the bed. Nina Harper had been in the local hospital for two days now, but it was only this afternoon that the doctors had permitted any visitors.

"She was tossing and turning a little while ago, but she didn't wake," Elizabeth whispered back.

The nurse smiled kindly. "Why don't you take a break?" she suggested. "Go get yourself a cup of coffee or a bite to eat. If she wakes up while you're gone, I'll have you paged."

Elizabeth hesitated, tempted by the suggestion. She'd been sitting by Nina's bedside for over two hours and was beginning to feel stiff and uncomfortable. She wouldn't mind stretching her legs and getting herself a cold drink. Elizabeth gave her friend another glance. Nina would almost look as though she were sleeping peacefully if it weren't for the ugly cuts and bruises on her face and arms.

She turned back to the nurse. "Thank you," Elizabeth said, "but I think I'll stay. I really

9

want to be here when she wakes up."

Nina was the best friend Elizabeth had made since she started at SVU, and she wanted Nina to know how much she cared about her.

"I understand." The nurse nodded sympathetically. "Would you like me to bring you a magazine?"

"I'm all right," Elizabeth said. She held up the notebook on her lap. "I have something to do."

After the door closed again, Elizabeth returned to her notebook, where she'd been trying to make sense out of what had happened to her friend by writing it all down. Two nights ago, Nina and Bryan Nelson, another friend of hers, had been walking back to her dorm from a meeting of the Black Student Union when they'd been brutally attacked by a group of men in dark clothes and masks. Nina had been lucky. She'd suffered a mild concussion and shock, but her other injuries hadn't been severe. Bryan was still in intensive care, and the doctors refused to say what they thought his chances were—not just of coming through without any permanent damage, but of coming through at all.

The unprovoked racial assault had stunned both the Sweet Valley University campus and the surrounding town, but no one was more upset than Elizabeth. The thought that something like this could happen in her country, at her college, and to someone like Nina troubled her deeply. She was determined to find out who was responsible and see that they were brought to justice.

"Elizabeth?" came a quiet, groggy voice. "What are you doing here?"

Nina was awake, blinking at the sunlight in the room. Elizabeth looked at her friend with one of her brightest smiles. "I was just in the neighborhood, so I thought I'd drop by," she joked. As she studied Nina's face her expression grew serious. "How are you feeling?"

"I've felt better," Nina answered, wincing a little in pain. "But considering the shape I was in a couple of days ago, I have to admit that I've also felt worse." She smiled, though her smile, like her voice, was weaker than it usually was. "At least being in here is good for my diet. I can't get to the snack vending machines, and the food is terrible. It's like airplane food, except there isn't any movie afterward."

Elizabeth laughed, relieved that Nina hadn't lost her sense of humor. "Not only are you losing weight, but purple is very becoming on you," she said, pointing to a bruise on Nina's arm.

"I guess it's too bad I'm probably not staying at SVU," said Nina. "I might start a new fad: the 'victim look.'"

The smile vanished from Elizabeth's lips. "What do you mean, you're probably not staying?"

Nina shrugged. "I mean I'm thinking of

11

transferring somewhere else at the end of the semester." She made a rueful face. "Somewhere where I'm not going to be beaten up because I happen to be black."

Elizabeth had expected Nina to be angry and even afraid, but she hadn't expected this. "But you can't leave," Elizabeth protested. "We've got to fight these people, Nina. We've got to expose them; we've got to make sure they pay for what they did."

"You can't expose men who hide behind masks," Nina argued. "I wouldn't even recognize their voices. How can we make them pay if we don't know who they are?"

Elizabeth moved to sit on the edge of the bed. "I have a pretty good idea who they are," she said. "Don't you remember what happened when Jessica went out with Danny Wyatt?"

At the beginning of the term, Jessica had gone to one of the big sorority parties with Danny Wyatt, an African-American student, and they'd been harassed so much by some of the fraternity brothers that they'd had to leave. Tom Watts, the aloof but brilliant chief reporter of the campus television station, had stopped the scene from becoming violent, but Elizabeth and Jessica had been taunted and threatened for several weeks after.

Nina looked at her intently. "You mean you think it was Peter Wilbourne and his Sigma buddies who did this to me and Bryan?"

Elizabeth nodded. "I do. They've never been very discreet about their racism." She tapped the notebook in her hand. "I've been writing down everything that's happened this autumn, starting with the Theta-Sigma party. If Tom will help me, I'm sure I can link them to the attack on you and Bryan."

"Maybe you can," Nina said. "But that still doesn't mean I have to be here to see your broadcast on WSVU. I can be at a college where I can work hard, get my degree, and mind my own business."

Elizabeth opened her mouth to argue that no one could afford to mind her or his own business in a case of brutal racism, but the words wouldn't come. *Who am I to tell Nina how she should act?* she asked herself. *She's the one in the hospital bed, not me. She's the one who could have been killed just for being herself.*

She placed her hand over Nina's. "I understand how you feel," she said softly. "I really do." Elizabeth did understand, and she certainly didn't blame Nina for not wanting to be the victim of hatred like that again. But Elizabeth silently promised herself not to stop until she'd discovered the truth. "You better stay in touch with me, though. I want to send you a video of my report when it's done."

*   *   *

Todd Wilkins jumped back as the basketball whizzed past his head. "Hey!" he cried. "Watch where you toss that ball."

Lauren Hill, his girlfriend, laughed. "What planet were you on, Todd? We're supposed to be shooting baskets. You're a million miles away."

Todd forced himself to smile. He wasn't going to admit to Lauren that he really had been a million miles away, or that the planet he'd been on was called Trouble.

"It's your fault," he lied. "I can't concentrate on my game when you're wearing those silk shorts." He put an arm around her shoulders, and kissed her on the cheek. "I'm used to playing with guys with hairy legs and knobby knees."

Still laughing, Lauren wriggled out of his grasp. "No excuses, Wilkins. You're not going to blame your bad playing on my legs."

Todd watched as she dashed across the court to retrieve the ball, but already his thoughts were wandering again. He'd told Lauren that morning that he'd been asked to appear before the board of trustees, that they were investigating the charges of preferential treatment given to university athletes, but he hadn't told her how worried he was.

When Elizabeth first told Todd she and Tom Watts were planning an investigation of the athletics department, he'd actually given her his blessing. What did he care? He wasn't doing anything illegal or immoral; he wasn't implicated. He could even remember laughing about it with some of the other jocks. "Elizabeth thinks she's Lois Lane," he'd joked.

The ball bounced off his shoulder. "Wilkins!" Lauren screamed. "Are you playing or not?"

But Todd wasn't laughing now. "Not!" he yelled back. "Let's go to the coffeehouse. I need something to drink."

Lauren came over and slipped her arm through his. "What's the matter?" she asked as they left the court. "Is it the investigation? Is that what's distracting you?"

Todd gave her a baleful look. "How did you guess?"

She smiled. "I've got good legs, but they're not that good."

"I'm sorry," Todd mumbled. "I don't want you to worry. I just can't get my mind off it."

Lauren's pretty face was blank. "Worry?" she asked. "Why should I worry? Nothing's going to happen to you. It's all going to be fine."

"You don't understand," Todd said, his eyes on the ground as they walked along. "Things have already happened. The whole team's been put on probation until the board's findings are in."

"So?" Lauren tossed her long red hair. "They're just going through the motions, Todd.

The school can't afford to shut down the jocks. You guys are too important."

"You mean we used to be too important. Now that the whole state's talking about an SVU 'scandal,' we're a liability. They're after blood. And I have this awful feeling some of it's going to be mine."

Lauren gave him a look he'd come to recognize. It was the look that settled over her face whenever the subject of Elizabeth came up, spoken or unspoken. Todd had broken up with Elizabeth, not the other way around, but Lauren was still jealous of her. If Lauren had ever said anything good about Todd's former girlfriend, it hadn't been when he was around.

"Well, you know who you have to thank for that," Lauren said sharply. "And even though you refuse to believe it, I'm sure I'm right about her. The only reason she decided to investigate the athletics department was because you dumped her."

Todd shook his head. "I can't believe that," he protested. "Elizabeth may not be perfect, but she's not vindictive, either."

Lauren smirked. "*Hell hath no fury like a woman scorned*, you know."

"Not Elizabeth," Todd said. "You don't know her the way I do."

"And I don't want to," Lauren said. She let go of his arm as they came to the entrance of

16

the coffeehouse, and he opened the door for her. "But maybe you don't know her as well as you thought you did," she said, sailing past him. "Maybe you only thought you knew her."

Todd followed Lauren into the cool darkness. *Maybe that's true,* he told himself. *Maybe I never really knew Elizabeth at all.*

There were several people he knew in the café. Todd got ready to smile in greeting. But where a few weeks ago they would all have waved to him or called him over, today not one of them even looked his way.

My life's going down the toilet, Todd thought, steering Lauren toward a corner booth. *And maybe Lauren's right. Maybe I do know who to thank.*

Enid Rollins, who now called herself Alexandra, slammed the door of Mark Gathers's brand-new Explorer so hard that for a second she was almost afraid the window would fall out. "Don't bother walking me to the door!" she shouted over her shoulder. "I know the way."

"That suits me just fine, Alex!" Mark shouted back. He gunned the engine.

He's not really going to leave me like this, she told herself. *He's just testing me. If I turn around, he'll be sitting there, staring at me, waiting for me to go back and make up.* But she wasn't going to give in that easily. She'd let him suffer for a few seconds, and then she'd turn around. She started counting to ten, very, very slowly. *One . . . two . . . three . . .*

The Explorer pulled out so fast that the tires squealed. By the time Enid turned around, Mark was halfway down the street.

Not bothering to try to stop the tears, Enid ran toward her dorm, mindless of the mascara running down her cheeks.

She'd been looking forward to her date with Mark all day. He'd been so preoccupied lately that she'd hardly seen him, and when she did see him, he was short-tempered and detached. Tonight, she'd promised herself, was going to be different. Tonight was going to be just like it had been when she and Mark first started going out together. Then, they'd sat up all night just talking about everything from politics to the dumb things they'd done when they were little. Then, all she had to do was smile and he was happy.

Enid crashed through the front door of her dorm and stormed down the hall. She took the stairs two at a time.

Now nothing she did made him happy. And he didn't want to talk about what was wrong. When she asked him what was bothering him, he said, "Nothing." When she pressed him, as she had tonight, he would either take her home early, complaining of a headache or a test in the morning, or blow up. Tonight Mark did both. First he'd yelled at her, telling her she wouldn't understand, and then he turned the car around and took her home.

When she finally reached her room, Enid threw herself on her bed and began to sob in earnest.

"Does he think I'm stupid?" she muttered. "Does he really think I don't know he's worried about the sports scandal?" How could he be so blind as to think she couldn't figure it out? Mark was one of the biggest jocks on campus; the minute the story had broken, suspicion had fallen on him.

Enid buried her face in her pillow. All she wanted was for Mark to confide in her. They'd been so close, so totally in love with each other, that Enid couldn't understand why he was keeping her away. He told her she was the most wonderful girl he'd ever met. He told her he'd never felt about anyone else the way he felt about her. But he wouldn't tell her why he was miserable and depressed.

"Everything was perfect until this happened," Enid told her empty room in a choked whisper. It was true, too. She'd never been so happy in her life. Good old, dull Enid Rollins had come to college, transformed herself into the glamorous and sexy Alexandra, and won the heart of one of the best-looking, most eligible guys in school. "And now it's ruined," she whispered. All because of that stupid scandal.

Enid sat up suddenly, hurling her pillow across the room. "All because of Elizabeth Wakefield." She picked up the little stuffed seal Mark had given her as a one-month anniversary present and threw that, too. "All because Elizabeth wanted to get even with me for not being her best friend anymore."

Celine Boudreaux was just about to leave Dickenson Hall when she spotted a familiar figure turning onto the path that led to the dorm. Tall and slender, dressed all in black, his long blond hair combed back and a white rose in his hand, there was only one man on campus it could be. And only one reason he would be coming to Dickenson Hall. Celine scowled. Although she had tried as hard as she could, she was not the reason William White was headed her way.

"Well, you're in for a disappointment," Celine murmured under her breath. "Because the Little Princess isn't here." She moved back into the foyer. "And I am."

Celine waited out of view until she saw William's shadow fall across the entryway, then she stepped forward, reaching out for the door just as it opened.

"Why, William," Celine cried, putting on her

sweetest and most seductive smile. "What a nice surprise."

Unless he wanted something from her, William's attitude toward her was usually one of undisguised contempt. When he wanted something, the contempt was at least slightly disguised.

"For you, maybe, Celine," he said in his deep, rich voice. "For me it's merely a surprise."

This evening, obviously, William didn't think he wanted anything from her.

Celine's smile didn't falter. "Maybe you're in for another surprise," she cooed, eyeing the rose. "Because if you're looking for Ms. Dull-as-Dishwater, she isn't here."

He tried to hide it, but she could see that she'd caught him off guard. Still smiling, she started to saunter past him.

One long, pale hand reached out and caught her by the wrist. "Where is she?" he asked. "We have a date."

"You mean *you* have a date." Celine shook her hand free. "Elizabeth's gone somewhere else."

He put out his arm, blocking her way. "Don't play games with me, Celine." Although his voice was quiet, there was no mistaking both the command and the threat in his words. "You know I hate it when you play games. Where is Elizabeth?"

Celine stared into those eyes, so light they

might have been made of glass—or ice. It amazed her that the worse William White treated her and the harder he pursued Elizabeth, the more she wanted him. Sometimes she wanted him so much, she thought it might really drive her crazy. *What's wrong with you?* she felt like screaming at him. *Can't you see we'd make a perfect couple? Can't you see that you and Elizabeth have as much in common as Dracula and Minnie Mouse?*

She was tempted to lie, to tell him that Elizabeth was out with another man, but she knew he'd know if she was lying. He could always tell. As Celine's old granny would have said, it took a liar to know one.

"She went to see Nina," Celine finally admitted.

The beautiful face frowned. "Nina?"

"Nina Harper," Celine said. "You know, the girl who was beaten up the other night."

"You mean that black girl?" He looked thoughtful. "I didn't know she was a friend of Elizabeth's."

Something in his voice caught Celine's attention: disapproval. William White didn't approve of Elizabeth being Nina's friend. Now, why was that? Celine pretended to brush something off her skirt so William wouldn't see the smile she couldn't quite suppress. Maybe William White was going to want something from her after all.

"I think she's become one of Elizabeth's

causes," she said matter-of-factly. She looked up, her expression innocent. "You know how Elizabeth gets; she's always trying to uncover something. I wouldn't be surprised if she wants to find out who attacked Nina and what's-his-name."

"Bryan Nelson," William said a little too quickly.

Celine smiled openly. Maybe it wasn't Nina whom William didn't approve of. Maybe he was worried that Elizabeth was really interested in Bryan. *Yes,* she told herself. *He's going to start being nice to me now.*

"Bryan Nelson," Celine repeated. She made a vague gesture. "I bet Elizabeth is thinking of making him and Nina her next cause."

William was watching her closely. "You know something, don't you?" he guessed. He took hold of the sleeve of her dress and gave it a tug. "Cough it up, Celine. What do you know?"

"Just that she's been jotting notes since it happened," Celine answered. She made a wry face. "It's a sure sign she's onto one of her stories."

He moved a little closer. "What kind of notes?"

Celine shrugged. "How would I know?"

Something that in someone else would have been warmth flickered in his eyes. "By reading them," he said.

Danny Wyatt looked up from his physics

book to find his roommate, Tom Watts, staring vacantly at the overhead light.

"What's the great brain thinking of now?" asked Danny. "The next Watts-Wakefield exposé?"

Tom, who had been thinking of Elizabeth Wakefield, but not in connection with their work at the television studio, turned his attention back to his sociology text so Danny wouldn't see him blush.

"Well?" Danny persisted when Tom didn't answer. "What's it going to be? You two have done the preferential treatment of jocks. And you've done the illegal hazing practices of the Sigma house. What's your new project going to be?"

Tom didn't look up. "I don't think there is going to be a new project," he said flatly.

"What do you mean, there isn't going to be a new project? You two are a great team. The rate you're going, you could be the youngest winners of the Pulitzer for investigative reporting ever."

Tom shrugged, but still refused to meet his roommate's eyes. Danny was right, of course. He and Elizabeth were a great team; that was the problem. When they were working together, the energy between them was so strong, it was almost electric. He and Elizabeth inspired and encouraged each other, developing ideas and theories ten times faster than either of them could have done alone.

24

But Tom didn't want to do another story with Elizabeth right now. He couldn't face it. He had fought his feelings as hard as he could, but the more he got to know Elizabeth, the stronger they became. Now she was involved with William White, and Tom couldn't bear working so closely with her knowing that they would never be more than friends.

"I thought I'd go back to working on my own," Tom said at last. "I like to work by myself. I don't want to be part of a team."

"Oh, right," Danny said. "You uncover two major scandals together, you save Winston Egbert's life, and you even get the athletics story aired on a major news show, but you don't want to be part of a team." He was silent for a few seconds. "This wouldn't have anything to do with the fact that Ms. Wakefield's been seeing a lot of William White lately, would it?" he asked, his voice almost wary.

One of the things Tom had always liked best about Danny was that he never invaded his privacy or asked personal questions. But since Elizabeth Wakefield had arrived on the scene, Danny's policy had changed. He had not only started asking personal questions, he was always giving Tom advice he didn't want.

Tom shoved his textbook aside and swiveled his chair around. "How many times do I have to tell you, Danny? I'm not interested in Elizabeth.

We're just work colleagues. That's all we've ever been, and that's all we ever will be."

"I'm glad to hear that," Danny answered. "You know, I've been giving it some thought, Tombo, and I think you're right. You and Elizabeth were never meant to be anything but friends. I see that now."

Tom stared at his best buddy, the man who had been urging him to ask Elizabeth Wakefield out since the beginning of the term. Apparently his policy had changed again. "You do?"

Danny nodded. "Yeah, I do."

"Well, I'm glad you finally agree with me," Tom said, trying to ignore the fact that he felt a little disappointed; part of him had been hoping for more of an argument. "Besides," Tom went on, "I'm not interested in having a relationship. I've got enough to keep me busy with the station."

Danny grinned. "You know what they say, Tombo . . ."

"I know, I know," Tom said quickly. "All work and no play—"

"No, that's not it," Danny said. "There's something else they say."

"Yeah? What's that?"

Danny smiled. "You never can tell."

Tom was still thinking about Elizabeth as he let himself into the television studio that night to catch up on some work. He hadn't seen her since the night the Sigmas got Winston drunk and sent him up on the roof of their fraternity house as part of his hazing. If he and Elizabeth hadn't figured out what was going on and turned up in time, Winston would almost certainly have fallen to his death.

He'd been so proud of Elizabeth that night—so proud of the two of them together. They'd gotten separated after the police came, but later she'd come to the studio to find him. He'd never seen her look so beautiful. He'd never wanted anything as much as he wanted to take her in his arms. And he had, for a moment. They were both so high from their triumph that for a split second they'd kissed. He was on the verge of telling her exactly how he felt.

Tom switched on the light with a sigh. Thank God he hadn't. He'd been just about to let those words out of his heart and into the air when William White showed up.

Tom kicked the door shut behind him. He could still see the smug, self-congratulatory look on William's face as he put his arm around Elizabeth's shoulders and steered her out of the studio.

After that, Elizabeth found out about Nina Harper being attacked, and since then she'd been spending all her free time at the hospital, waiting to see her friend. "Which is just as well," Tom muttered to himself as he crossed to his desk.

At least it had given him a little time to think about what to do. He knew it wasn't going to be easy to resist the temptation to work with Elizabeth, especially when they were still trying to work out what was behind the Sigmas' dangerous hazing practices, but he was going to have to force himself.

Tom switched on his computer. As he started to sit down he noticed a plain white envelope on his chair.

That's strange, Tom thought. *That wasn't there when I locked up this afternoon.* He watched the envelope for a few seconds, almost as though it were going to explode.

He gave himself a shake. "What's wrong with you?" he asked himself. "It's just an envelope. It probably fell out of your desk or something."

As soon as he picked it up he knew it wasn't just an envelope. There was a letter inside it. Tom ripped open the seal and removed a single sheet of paper. The letter, if you could call it a letter, was made up of words cut from magazines. The message was short and to the point:

In case you and the blond were thinking of doing a story on that troublemaker Bryan Nelson and his little friend, don't. Have you forgotten your promise? We aren't going to tell you twice.

At the bottom, instead of a signature, someone had stamped a broken star.

Tom collapsed in his seat. It had been so long since he'd seen that insignia that he'd managed to forget it existed. Just as he'd managed to forget about the secret society it stood for. That is, until Elizabeth thought she saw a connection between it and the "accidental" deaths from fraternity hazings that had been going on since the fifties.

Tom stared at the paper in his hand. He hadn't expected this.

"I guess the broken star isn't the only thing that slipped my mind," Tom told himself. He'd also forgotten how ruthless and determined the society could be.

He folded the letter and put it back in its envelope. And he'd forgotten that there was no way in a million years the society would ever forget him.

Chapter Two

Danny came through the door of the coffee-house and headed straight for the table for two in the back. Isabella Ricci was already there, her head bent over the menu. They'd known of each other for a long time, but the first time they'd talked was when he was going out with Jessica Wakefield, and Isabella and Jessica were roommates.

A few weeks ago they'd met again at the television studio, and ever since, a friendship had sprung up between them. Besides the fact that they had similar tastes in music, movies, and food, they had soon discovered that they had something else in common: Tom. Danny loved Tom like a brother; Isabella wanted to be Tom's girlfriend.

As though she instinctively knew he was there, Isabella looked up from the menu as Danny neared the table.

"Hi!" she called out. She waved, and the gold bracelets on her arm jangled.

Danny waved back. Not for the first time, it struck him that seeing Isabella smile was a lot like watching dawn break on a beautiful day. "Hi, yourself." He slid into the chair across from her, dropping his book bag on the floor. "Have you made up your mind?" He showed her his watch. "I gave you five extra minutes."

Ever since he and Isabella had started having lunch together once or twice a week, her inability to order food had become a standing joke between them. It took her at least half an hour to decide on what she wanted, and even then she almost always changed her mind.

Isabella laughed. "Pasta salad," she said decisively. "Pasta salad and raspberry iced tea."

Danny picked up his own menu. "You're sure?" he asked, grinning back. "Pasta salad?"

She nodded. "Absolutely."

Danny scanned the list of sandwiches.

"Well?" Isabella prompted.

He shrugged. "I don't know. I feel kind of torn between the Greek melt and the super sub."

"Not that, you space brain," hissed Isabella. "What about Tom?"

"Tom hates olives," Danny said, pretending that he didn't understand her. "He wouldn't like either the melt or the sub."

"Stop teasing me." She kicked him under

the table. "Did you talk to Tom?"

Relenting, Danny looked up with a smile. "Yes, I talked to him." He shook his head. "Not that it's easy. Getting Tom to talk about anything personal is like getting Jessica to talk about quantum mechanics."

"Danny!" Isabella groaned in frustration. "What are you trying to do, drive me crazy? What did Tom say? Is he interested in Elizabeth?"

Danny laughed. There was something about winding up Isabella that gave him a lot of pleasure. "He says he's not," he admitted. "He even said that he's not going to work on his next big story with her. I think any interest he did have in Elizabeth is over now that she's seeing William White."

"Well, thank God for that." Isabella leaned back in her chair, her beautiful eyes sparkling. "I for one hope Elizabeth and William are very happy together." She giggled impishly. "And for a long, long time."

Danny signaled the waitress. "Now all we have to do is find a way of getting you and Tom together." It was a problem he'd been giving some thought to over the last week or two.

"Maybe I should just ask him out," Isabella said. "You know, go for the direct approach."

"Uh-uh." Danny folded his hands on the table and leaned toward her. "The direct approach isn't going to work with Tom. If you ask him out, he'll say no, and then he'll avoid you for the rest of the term. Take it from me, you have to sneak up on Tom. His resistance is high."

"What are you suggesting? That I lurk in doorways and alleys, waiting for him to walk by so I can jump out and surprise him?"

Danny smiled. "No, I'm suggesting that you just happen to be in the pizza parlor tomorrow night at about eight thirty."

Isabella gazed back at him quizzically.

"Tuesdays, Tom and I work out at the gym after he's through at the station, and then we usually go for something to eat."

"You're a genius!" Isabella reached across the table and squeezed his hand. "I'll be there."

"You ready to order?"

They both looked up to see the waitress standing beside them, her pencil poised.

"The lady will have a pasta salad and a raspberry iced tea," said Danny. "And I'll have the Greek melt and a lemonade."

The waitress picked up the menus. "Pasta salad and raspberry iced tea," she repeated, checking her order form. "Greek melt and a pink lemonade."

"Wait a minute," said Isabella, snatching her menu from the waitress's hand. "How's the sesame chicken?"

If Tom wasn't in a class, in his room, or eating,

there was one place he was likely to be, and that was at his desk at the television station. As Danny often kidded him, some people worked in order to live, but Tom Watts lived in order to work.

Today Tom was taking advantage of the free hour he had between his advanced journalism course and a political science seminar to run through the roster of suggestions for upcoming WSVU broadcasts.

"A follow-up on the athletics scandal," he read out loud. He tossed the card onto the "yes" pile.

"A piece on the all-fraternity charity event." He tossed it with the "maybes."

"A profile on Parents' Day." Tom groaned. What could be fluffier than a profile on Parents' Day? he wondered. He was supposed to be running a hard-edged news program, not a community bulletin board. He flipped the card into the garbage.

"If you don't like that, how about a special on racism on campus, then?"

Tom didn't have to turn to know who had come into the studio behind him, but he turned anyway. Elizabeth was standing in the doorway, her books against her chest and her face bright with excitement.

"I didn't hear you come in." Tom laughed uneasily. He'd been halfheartedly hoping that she wouldn't suggest following up on what had happened to Nina and Bryan, even though he knew it was a natural for her. Two of the things he loved most about Elizabeth were her hatred of injustice and her strong sense of loyalty.

Elizabeth came toward him. "Well, here I am," she announced. "Ready and raring to go."

Tell her, he urged himself as he watched her draw closer. *Just tell her you don't have the time to do it now, and she can't do it alone.* Tom cleared his throat. He cleared his throat again. It was one thing telling Danny that he didn't want to work with Elizabeth. It was another telling Elizabeth. Especially when she was staring at him with that intelligent glint in her blue-green eyes and that melt-your-heart smile.

She stopped only inches from him. "Well?" she prodded. "When do we start?"

Tom focused his gaze on a desk behind her. "You want to do a piece on campus racism?" he managed to choke out.

Elizabeth put her books on the floor and hopped up on the desk. "That's right," she said. "I want to bring it out in the open—it's the only way we'll ever stop it." Her cheeks glowed with color and her voice became more passionate. "And more specifically," she went on, "I'm determined to find out who attacked Nina and to see that they're brought to justice."

Tom was beginning to understand just how unreliable his own heart was. No matter what he

36

wanted it to do—no matter what he told it to do—it had gotten into the habit of doing something else. Now, when he wanted it to harden itself against Elizabeth, it was leaping all over the place. *Way to go, Tom!* his heart was shouting. *Tell her yes and let's get started!*

"What about Nina?" Tom asked, deciding to stall both Elizabeth and his heart. "What does she think about your idea?"

Elizabeth frowned. "Nina doesn't want to have anything to do with it," she admitted. "She's transferring as soon as the semester's over."

"Then maybe you should drop the idea," Tom said, trying not to sound too relieved. "If Nina—"

Elizabeth interrupted him. "Nina's scared, Tom. She's terrified out of her wits." She leaned forward, the frown replaced by a look of determination. "Don't you see? That's why we have to do this story. If everyone keeps quiet, the hatred and violence will just grow and grow."

Why does she always have to echo my own thoughts? Tom wondered. *Why does she have to be so committed and so smart?*

"I know, Elizabeth, but—"

"But what?" She slid from the desk, standing directly in front of him. "We know who's behind it, Tom. It's Peter Wilbourne and his Sigma thugs. We've already got them on the run because of their illegal hazing. What are we waiting for? Let's blow those creeps wide open. Let's tell the world what vicious bigots they are."

Tom took a deep breath. Even if he hadn't resolved to keep her out of his life as much as possible, he couldn't let her do the story now, not after that warning from the secret society. When they said they weren't going to tell him twice, they meant it.

On the other hand, he didn't want to tell her about the letter if he didn't have to. Knowing Elizabeth, a little thing like a death threat wasn't going to put her off. He was worried it would only make her more determined.

"I don't think it's really what we should be focusing on right now," he managed to say. "It's too explosive. Maybe we should let things settle down a little."

"Settle down?" She sounded as though that was the most contemptible idea she'd ever heard.

"We've caused a lot of trouble with the sports scandal and the piece on Winston," Tom answered. "Let's face it, Elizabeth, the university might not be so willing to fund us next semester if we don't start doing something more positive."

Elizabeth's eyes widened. "Am I hearing right?" she asked the ceiling. "Did Tom Watts just say we should go soft so we don't upset the powers that be?"

Another thing Tom loved about Elizabeth was her spirit. Usually. "I'm not saying we should go soft," he snapped. "I'm just saying we should wait a little while."

She glared back at him. "Are you saying you won't do the story?"

"It's not that, Elizabeth. It's just that—"

"What?" Elizabeth demanded. "What are you saying?"

Tom threw his hands in the air. "All right!" he yelled, his voice louder than he'd intended. "I'm saying we can't do the story. Even if we weren't risking having our funding cut off, it's too dangerous. It's—"

"Well, let me tell you something, Tom Watts." The golden hair swung as Elizabeth grabbed up her books and started marching across the room. "If you won't do it with me, I'll do it alone. You may be the boss around here, but that doesn't mean you can prevent me from discovering the truth." She stopped at the door and turned back, her eyes flashing. "And when I discover it, you can't prevent me from making it public, either. Maybe you're afraid of upsetting people, but there are dozens of papers and television stations that aren't."

Tom watched her bang out of the studio, and then he put his head on his desk. *Now what?* he silently asked himself. *Why does she have to be so incredibly stubborn? Why do I have to love her for it?*

* * *

Winston Egbert was sitting in the common room of Oakley Hall, watching game shows on the television and thinking about depression. Ever since he'd resigned from the Sigmas after the whole hazing debacle, Winston had been depressed. Even though he'd finally realized how heinous Peter Wilbourne, the president of the fraternity, really was—and how close they'd come to killing him—he couldn't help feeling disappointed that he would never be a big man on campus now. Not if he stayed at SVU for the rest of his life.

Everyone has their own way of dealing with depression, Winston thought. He reached in the cardboard box beside him, took out another bag of salt-and-vinegar chips—his third—and ripped it open. *And this is mine. Darkness, solitude, people dancing across the TV dressed as bottles of ketchup, and food with lots of artificial ingredients.*

"What are you doing sitting in here with the curtains closed, Winnie?"

The sudden burst of light as the door opened and the sudden sound of Denise Waters' voice only feet away almost knocked Winston off the couch.

Denise strode past him and tore open the curtains. "Well?" she demanded, turning to face him. "What are you doing, Winston? Impersonating a slug?"

Winston concentrated on picking up the

chips he'd spilled. "I don't have any afternoon classes," he mumbled.

"What?" Denise bellowed.

It suddenly struck Winston that for a lovely, charming, and totally feminine woman, Denise really could shout like a hog-caller when she wanted.

"I can't hear you above this stupid show." She left her post by the window and snapped off the TV set. "Now," she said, coming over and throwing herself beside him on the sofa. "What are you doing here? It's a beautiful day, the sun is shining, the world is filled with exciting things to do . . ." She snatched the bag of chips from his hand with two fingers. "And you're holed up in here eating junk food." Her brilliant blue eyes bored into his muddy brown ones. "Why?"

Winston looked at the cellophane bag. "Umph," he grunted.

"Look me in the face," Denise ordered. "Why?"

He looked her in the face. It was one of the most beautiful faces Winston had ever seen. It was a face that drifted through his dreams and haunted his waking hours. It was a face he loved. Winston's heart sank a little lower. Now that he was back to being good old Winston, nerd and nobody, he would never be able to tell Denise how he felt.

"I'm sulking," he whispered.

"Sulking?" Denise dropped the chips. "Sulking about what?"

Winston's eyes shifted nervously. "I can't tell you," he mumbled.

Denise leaned back. "Why not?" she asked more gently. "I thought we were friends."

"We are friends," Winston said quickly. "But you'll laugh if I tell you. You'll think I'm a jerk."

One hand, so perfect it looked as if it must have been carved out of marble, touched his shoulder. The hand wasn't marble; it was as warm and gentle as the breath of a baby. "No, I won't, Winston. Tell me why you're sulking."

Winston stared at her shell-pink nails, getting up his courage. *Go on*, he urged himself. *She's right, you're friends. And Denise has stuck by you through everything.* He caught his breath. "Because now that I'm out of the Sigmas, I'll never be a big important guy," he said in a rush. "That's why. Because I'm still Winston the clown, just like I was in high school."

There were several seconds of a pure and profound silence, and then that silence was broken by the equally pure sound of Denise Waters laughing herself silly.

"You're right," she gasped. "You are a jerk."

Winston felt himself turn several shades of red, each one darker than the last. *Please don't let me cry*, he begged. *That's all I ask; don't let me cry in front of Denise.*

Suddenly her hands were on his shoulders. "What is wrong with you, Winnie?" she asked, giving him a shake. "How many times do we have to tell you? Nobody cares if you're a Sigma. That's not important. You're one of the nicest guys I've ever known. All of the girls in the dorm think so." She shook him again. "You're a jerk because that isn't enough for you. Because you think you've got to impress everybody."

Winston opened his mouth. He closed his mouth. He opened it again. "Really? That's why I'm a jerk?"

Denise nodded. "Yes, that's why you're a jerk." She got to her feet, tugging him after her. "Come on," she said. "I'm free this afternoon, too. Why don't we go play a game of tennis or shoot some pool?"

Winston wasn't sure he could walk, never mind run after a ball. "I've never really played pool," he said lamely.

Denise hooked her arm through his and started pulling him toward the door. "Then maybe it's time you learned."

"Can you believe that?" Elizabeth's voice rose indignantly above the gentle purring of the engine. Her eyes were on the side of William's face as he drove the silver convertible through the twilight. She'd been furious ever since her talk with Tom, but she'd had no one to share her rage with until now. "I just don't understand him. We worked on the sports story together, we worked on the fraternity story together. It's not like they weren't difficult and dangerous. But now he refuses to do this one. And it's probably the most important story of all!"

"I really don't see what the big deal is," William said. "It's just some more Sigma nonsense, and you've already nailed them."

Ordinarily, Elizabeth would have been astounded to hear a friend of hers describe violence and racism as "no big deal"—astounded and offended. Tonight, however, she was so upset about Tom, she barely registered the remark.

"But why doesn't Tom want me to do the piece?" she persisted. "He knows I'm good. He knows I'm committed."

William pulled to a stop at the light and looked over at her. In the shadows of the evening, the tiny diamond in his left ear was the only thing she could see clearly.

"Maybe Tom's jealous of you," William said. His lips formed the suggestion of a smile. "After all, Tom was the star reporter around here until you arrived, Elizabeth. Maybe he's worried that you're going to surpass him."

For the first time since she'd stormed out of the newsroom, Elizabeth was speechless. She stared back at William. "But—but that's ridiculous," she spluttered. "Tom isn't like that.

Tom's—" She broke off when she realized that she was about to say that Tom had more integrity and character than any man she'd ever known. Her instincts told her that this wasn't the kind of thing William wanted to hear.

"Tom's what?" William asked.

Elizabeth blinked, wishing she could see into those cool, almost-colorless eyes. Although William's voice was as rich and even as ever, she thought she detected something hard and sharp beneath its surface.

"Tom's a professional," she answered. "He wouldn't jeopardize a story like this because of petty jealousy."

The light changed and William threw the car into gear. "Wouldn't he?"

"No," Elizabeth said. "No, he wouldn't."

As effortlessly as smoke rising from a chimney, the convertible began to climb into the hills.

"How do you know that, Elizabeth?" William asked. "How can you be so sure?"

Elizabeth stared out the windshield as the houses fell beneath them and the sky drew nearer. The truth was that she didn't know how she knew. Tom Watts was not a person who gave himself away easily. With Tom, you could only get so close; and to be honest with herself, Elizabeth had to admit that Tom didn't allow anyone very close at all. But still, she was sure. Whatever Tom's reasons for wanting to keep her off the story, jealousy wasn't one of them.

"I've worked with Tom," Elizabeth answered. "I know him. I—"

William interrupted. "In that case, you must know him a lot better than I thought." The car took a curve a little too sharply. "Do you?"

"Do I what?" she asked as they pulled into an overview high over the valley.

He cut the engine. "Do you know Tom Watts better than I thought?"

Elizabeth looked into William's eyes, as hard as a glacier. He was easily the most beautiful man she had ever seen. He was also intelligent, sensitive, kind, stylish, elegant, well mannered, wealthy, considerate, and attentive—everything a woman could possibly want. *Tell him now,* Elizabeth urged herself. *Tell him that as much as you like him, you just don't have that kind of feelings for him* . . . The kind of feelings she had for Tom. But something in the way he was watching her stopped her.

She shook her head. "No," she said. "No, I don't know him that well."

Something lightened in his expression, but he didn't speak.

"It's just my instincts," Elizabeth explained, anxious to fill up the silence. "That's all."

William laughed, sounding relieved. "Women's intuition, right?" He got out of the car and came around to her side. He opened the door and, taking her hand, pulled her to her feet. "Well, I'm glad to hear that," he said softly. "I was beginning to wonder . . ."

He was standing so close to her that Elizabeth could feel his breath on her cheek.

She stepped back suddenly, looking around. "So where are we?" she asked, keeping her voice light. "Why have you brought me here?"

Still holding on to her, he led her to the edge of the cliff. "I wanted you to see this," William told her. His tone became slightly acid. "I didn't realize we were going to be spending the evening talking about Tom Watts and current events." He gestured below them to where the lights of the town glittered like jewels and the ocean stretched on forever. "I wanted to lay the world at your feet."

Nina lay in her bed, staring at the television screen suspended from the opposite wall. A sitcom that usually made her laugh was on, but it might as well have been a documentary on World War II for all the fun she was getting out of it.

Down the corridor came the sound of other televisions, and of nurses talking softly and orderlies hurrying by, pushing wheelchairs and carts, but Nina paid no attention to them, either. As happy as she'd been to see Elizabeth, the visit had left her more confused than she'd been before.

Was Elizabeth right? Should she stay at SVU and fight; should she stand up to those thugs? Or were Nina's parents right? Was the way to achieve equality not by protesting and challenging but by jumping into the mainstream and swimming as hard as you could? The purple bruises glistened against the brown of Nina's skin as tears streamed silently down her face.

"I can't believe this," Nina whispered to the empty room. "It isn't fair. I had so many plans . . ."

She should never have joined the BSU. That was where she'd made her first mistake. If she hadn't joined, she wouldn't have been out that night and none of this would have happened. Instead of getting all excited about standing up and fighting ignorance and hatred, she should have stayed in her room, studying, just as she always had. She wanted to be a success in life, not a martyr. She wanted to have a nice house and a nice car and all the things that mattered—all the things that meant you'd made it. She didn't want to end up the headline on a daily newspaper: STRAIGHT-A STUDENT MURDERED IN RACIST ATTACK. It was all Bryan's fault. It was because she'd listened to him.

Bryan. Up until this moment, Nina had managed not to think about him. It hadn't been that hard. She'd been in such a state of shock and in so much pain the first day or two. But now she couldn't stop herself from thinking about him.

"Oh, Bryan . . ." Nina sobbed.

A commercial for milk came on, but Nina hardly noticed. Instead of a herd of singing and dancing cows, she was seeing Bryan the way he looked that night before the assault. Strong and handsome; confident and determined. Fresh tears glazed her cheeks. Nina knew that Bryan had been badly hurt in the beating. The doctors and nurses had refused to tell her how badly, but she'd taken that to mean his condition was serious. Nina wiped her eyes with the edge of the sheet. She was afraid to ask about Bryan in case they told her something awful—that he was in a coma or would never walk again. In case they told her he was dead.

As the cows faded from the screen the door to her room slowly opened. Nina turned. Nurse Alvarez was standing in the doorway, a big smile on her face.

The feeling Nina had feared she might never experience again exploded in her heart: joy. *It's Bryan!* she thought. *She's come to tell me Bryan's going to be all right!*

"I've got some good news for you," Nurse Alvarez announced.

"When can I see him?" Nina blurted.

"Him?" Nurse Alvarez looked puzzled. "You mean *them*, don't you?"

"Them?" Nina had been so sure the news was about Bryan that she couldn't imagine what the nurse was talking about.

"Your parents."

As the nurse approached the bed Nina realized for the first time that she was carrying a telephone.

"We finally reached them," Nurse Alvarez explained. She plugged in the phone. "They're at a conference in Geneva." She held out the receiver. "Here," she whispered. "It's your mother."

Nina put the phone to her ear.

"Nina?" Her mother's voice enveloped her like a blanket. "Nina, honey, are you all right?"

Nina nodded, and then, realizing that her mother couldn't see her nodding, said, "Yes. Yes, Mom. I'm all right."

"Thank God for that." There were several bleeps and a crackle and the sound of someone talking in the background.

"Mom?" Suddenly Nina was overwhelmed with homesickness.

As if hearing her thoughts, her mother came back on the line. "Your father's going to have to stay here, sweetheart, but as soon as I've finished my business I'm coming to take you home."

Celine lit another cigarette and leaned back against the pillows she'd piled against the wall.

"This is what I call a perfect evening," she said, blowing smoke toward Elizabeth's side of the room. "Peace, quiet, and the Little Princess's writings to keep me amused."

She smiled to herself as she opened the spiral notebook Elizabeth used for her work at WSVU. If Celine were Elizabeth, she'd dust everything she owned for fingerprints at least once a day.

"But I'm not Little Miss Truth-and-Justice," Celine commented, flicking through the pages. "I'm not that stupid and trusting, thank God." She yawned as she read Elizabeth's neat, precise handwriting. "Or that boring."

Really, Celine asked herself as she plowed through the notes Elizabeth had taken for her story about fraternity hazing. *What sort of life could a person have who'd rather be sitting in a library, reading through old newspapers, than be out partying?*

A tiny frown disturbed the perfection of Celine's beautiful face as she remembered that the sort of life Elizabeth had included going out on romantic dates with William White.

"But not for much longer, my pretty," Celine whispered. "Not for much longer."

At last she reached the newest section of notes. Celine read quickly. There was nothing here that she didn't already know. Nothing that would interest William White, that was. All Elizabeth had done was plot out every racist or possibly racist incident that had occurred since the beginning of the semester. The harassment of Danny and Jessica at the Theta-Sigma party.

The way the Sigmas had taunted Jessica and Elizabeth through the first weeks of school. The scene at the Halloween dance when Danny finally stood up to his persecutors and someone almost attacked Jessica outside Xavier Hall. The assault on Nina and Bryan. Most interesting of all was how many times the names Peter Wilbourne and Sigma appeared.

"Peter, Peter, pumpkin eater . . ." Celine recited, letting the notebook drop to her lap and stubbing out her cigarette in the ashtray at the side of her bed. She smiled, a slow, self-satisfied smile. Maybe William White wasn't the only one who would appreciate knowing what Elizabeth was up to. . . .

It was a picture-perfect spring day. Sunlight shone rainbowlike through the stained-glass windows of the small white church, and the aisles were decked with white ribbons and flowers in the most delicate shades of pink. At the front of the church, more flowers spilled across the altar and the handsome groom in his black morning coat glanced nervously toward the vestibule. There was a soft buzz of excited conversation as the guests in all their finery filed into the pews.

Suddenly the rich strains of organ music filled the air. A hush fell on the crowd and all heads turned. For a moment there was nothing at the back of the church but a curtain of light, and then, her arm through the arm of her proud father, the bride appeared at the top of the center aisle. There was a gasp of appreciation as she stood there for a heartbeat, more beautiful than a princess in a fairy tale, more lovely than a vision in a dream.

Then, her heart beating like a thousand drums, the young bride raised her head, her eyes on the man who gazed at her adoringly from the front of the church, and began to walk slowly but surely toward him. This is my most perfect moment, *she told herself as she moved toward her destiny.* This is the day I'll never forget . . .

"Michael McAllery and Jessica Wakefield?" asked a soft but businesslike voice.

Jessica came back to reality with a jolt at the sound of their names. She looked up to see the small, smiling blond woman in the rhinestone-studded dress who had greeted them when they arrived beckoning them into the next room.

Michael was already on his feet. "That's us," he said, pulling Jessica after him.

As Jessica followed him inside, Mrs. Moppet, the minister's wife, reached out and took Jessica's motorcycle helmet from her. "Here, sweetheart," she said, thrusting a bouquet of artificial flowers into her hands. "Some of the chapels don't go in for anything fancy—you know, it's all wham, bam, thank you, ma'am—but I think these make a nice, romantic touch."

Jessica's eyes moved from the small room crammed with old furniture and sleeping cats to the limp, slightly dirty bunch of silk roses in her hands. *Well, I'm not going to forget this day in a hurry,* she told herself sourly. *It'll be engraved in my mind till the day I die.*

Mike put his arm around her as they came to a stop in front of the Reverend Douglas Moppet, minister of the Forever After Chapel. "Nervous?" Mike whispered.

"A little." Jessica jumped as a paw suddenly reached out from the shelf above her and swiped at the barrette in her hair.

Michael gave her a squeeze. "Me too. Somehow, I don't think I ever thought I'd be doing this."

Who did? Jessica wondered. Getting married in a pet store cum junk shop wasn't exactly the kind of thing you predicted or planned for.

Mrs. Moppet, her arms now filled with something large and orange, took her place at the side of the gilt desk that acted as the Reverend Moppet's altar.

"Marlowe here will be the best man," she said, holding up the wriggling cat. "And I'll be your witness and the maid of honor."

Jessica's heart, already somewhere in the vicinity of her knees, sank a little lower. She could accept the idea of not being married in a church, and she could live with wearing faded jeans and Mike's old Sturgis, South Dakota, T-shirt instead of a long white dress, but she would never get used to the fact that on this, the biggest day of her life, Elizabeth wasn't here to share it with her.

For one awful moment, the urge came over her to leave. *Just throw these stupid flowers away and run,* she told herself. *You don't have to do this. You can still change your mind.*

The Reverend Moppet cleared his throat. Mike took her hand, weaving his fingers between hers, holding her so tightly that she couldn't tell where her body ended and his began. His palm was sweating, and she was sure she could hear the beating of his heart.

Jessica looked into Mike's eyes, and suddenly all her doubts and regrets vanished. Time stood still and the Moppets, their cats, and the cheerless chapel all faded away. All Jessica could see was Mike. All she cared about was him. Him and their love.

This was right. This was her destiny. The sounds of the ceremony were drowned out by the clamor of her own passionate heart, a sound much louder and richer than a hundred organs playing "Here Comes the Bride" could ever be.

The next thing Jessica heard was her own voice saying "I do" as Mike slipped his silver-and-turquoise ring onto her finger.

55

Chapter Three

Mike lifted his glass and tapped it against Jessica's. "Here's to you, Mrs. McAllery," he said, his eyes staring into hers. "Thank you for making me the happiest man in the world."

Thrilled by the sound of her new name, Jessica leaned over and gave him a kiss. "Anytime," she whispered. "All you have to do is ask."

He kissed her back. "All right," he said. "Make me even happier. How about a wedding dance while the feast is being prepared?"

Jessica laughed. "Dance?" She looked around. If she'd always dreamt of a formal white wedding, she'd also always imagined a lavish reception and a honeymoon in some faraway, exotic place like Tahiti or Bali. But their honeymoon was a night camping out and a romantic dinner in Jack's Desert Rose Diner. "Here?"

He put down his beer. "Sure, here. It's our

wedding night, Mrs. McAllery. We have to dance." Getting to his feet, Mike reached into his pocket and pulled out a handful of change. "What'll it be? Something old or something new?"

Jessica followed him over to the jukebox. "But we can't dance here, Mike," she hissed. "There's no room. They'll get annoyed."

"Something old," Mike said. "Something old and suitable for the occasion."

"But Mike—"

He swung around, looking over to where Jack himself was turning their burgers and the waitresses were picking up orders. "Does anybody mind if my bride and I have our wedding dance here?" he called out.

Both waitresses stopped what they were doing.

"Your bride?" cried the blonde. "You mean you two just got hitched?"

Mike grinned. "That's right." He pointed to the clock over the counter. "Exactly five hours, twenty-seven minutes, and thirty-three seconds ago."

"I'm going to get all misty," said the red-head. "I really am."

Jack banged on the counter. "Not only can you two dance!" he shouted. "But the two double-cheeseburger platters are on the house."

"You see?" Mike said. He shoved two quarters into the old Wurlitzer and punched some buttons. "I told you it would be all right."

"What a husband," Jessica said, a tingle running through her at the unaccustomed use of the word.

Elvis Presley's voice singing "Love Me Tender" filled the diner. It was their song. Back at the grill, Jack began to sing along.

Mike took her in his arms. "Are you happy?" he asked. "Are you really and truly happy?"

Jessica pressed herself against him. "There's no woman I would want to change places with," she murmured, overcome with happiness. "Not one in the entire world."

Nina slowly opened her eyes. Daylight was streaming in the hospital window and her mother was just coming into the room, her arms filled with shopping bags.

"Good morning, darling," she called brightly. "How are you feeling?"

"All right," Nina mumbled. She'd thought that the nightmares she'd been having since the attack would disappear once her mother arrived and took charge, but they hadn't. They still haunted her nights, causing her to sleep fitfully and wake almost as tired as if she hadn't slept at all. "Fine."

Grace Harper set down her bags and began pulling things out. "I know you're getting out of here tomorrow, but I decided you've had enough hospital food," she said briskly. "I bought fresh rolls, fruit, and yogurt."

Nina made a face. "But I don't like yogurt."

Her mother snapped the lid from a container. "Never mind you don't like yogurt; it's good for you." She produced a bag of rolls and a tub of butter and set them on the tray.

"I can't eat that," Nina protested. "Elizabeth and I are on a diet."

"Oh, Nina, don't be ridiculous," her mother told her in what Nina thought of as her boardroom voice. "Your friend Elizabeth may be on a diet, but you need to get your strength back, not lose weight." She paused in her unpacking to give Nina an appraising look. "Don't you want to wash up before you eat?" she asked. "Shall I run you a bath?"

Nina started to say that she could run her own bath, but her mother was still talking.

"We'll have you back on your feet in no time," she was saying. "Back on your feet and safe at home."

Home. Nina sighed inwardly. When her mother had first suggested taking her home, she'd thought it was a great idea. Now she wasn't so sure. As nice as it was to be fussed over, after only a day of her mother's attention she was beginning to feel like a little kid again. Besides that, Nina knew that the attention wouldn't last. After she was home for a day or two, her parents would be too busy with their jobs and social engagements to spend more than half an hour a day with her.

"I'm sure your father can pull some strings to get you into temporary classes at the state college," Grace continued. "Then next semester you can transfer to one of the Ivy League schools. Princeton, or maybe Harvard." She gave Nina a determined smile. "Which is where you would have gone in the first place, if you'd listened to us."

Nina pushed back the covers. "I'll go get washed," she said obediently.

In the bathroom Nina sat on the edge of the tub, wondering what she was going to do. As much as she wanted to leave Sweet Valley University and forget what had happened, she didn't want to go to Princeton or Harvard. Not that there was any point in telling her mother that again.

Nina had argued with her parents all through high school about what college she would go to. They'd wanted her to go to one of the prestigious, East Coast schools where she would meet people who could help further her career. Nina had wanted to go to a school where she would meet people interested in more than just making money. In the end, she'd made her parents promise that if she had the highest grade-point average of her class, they'd let her choose her college. That's how she'd come to SVU.

When Nina came back, her mother was sitting in the chair beside her bed, watching the news on the television.

"That young nurse dropped by to see you," she said, not taking her eyes from the stock market report. "She said something about a friend of yours. That he's out of danger."

"Bryan?" Nina couldn't keep the sudden rush of joy out of her voice. "She said Bryan's all right?"

Grace Harper looked up at her, her expression somber. "Is that the boy you were with?" she wanted to know. "Is that the radical?"

Nina was too happy to pay any attention to her mother's words. "When did she say I could see him?" she asked eagerly. "Can I see him now?"

"See him?" Nina's mother laughed. "After all the trouble he's caused you?" She turned back to the set. "If you want my opinion, I don't think you should ever see him again."

Elizabeth put down her pen and looked over the top of her study carrel. Just across from her was the door to the microfiche room. *My home away from home,* she thought wryly, remembering all the hours she'd recently spent in there, researching material for her and Tom's exposé on fraternity hazing.

The soft sounds of the library stopped as Elizabeth stared at the door. Something was trying to get through to her. Something important that she'd forgotten.

Microfiche, she repeated to herself. *Fraternity . . . Hazing . . . Research . . .*

"Bingo!"

From behind her, several voices hissed, "Shhh!"

Elizabeth didn't normally call out "Bingo!" in the library study area, but today she didn't even apologize. She'd thought of something incredibly important. Something so important she couldn't believe she'd ever let it slip her mind. But she'd been so determined to break the Sigmas because of her dislike of Peter Wilbourne and the way they'd treated Winston that she'd overlooked her own theory about the accidental deaths at Sigma house: they were actually being used to distract attention from something else. Something even bigger and more frightening than the fraternity.

"And it nearly worked this time, too," Elizabeth told herself as she gathered up her books and raced out of the library. "The secret society. How could I not have thought of this?" As she crossed the quad to Tom's office, Elizabeth could hear Tom trying to persuade her to drop the story completely. Elizabeth quickened her pace. Maybe she hadn't been thinking about the secret society, but it suddenly hit her that Tom probably had. Of course! That's why he was so worried about investigating this story.

Elizabeth quietly opened the door to the studio. As usual, Tom was at the computer, his back to her and so absorbed in whatever he was working on that he didn't hear her come in.

For a second Elizabeth stood there, watching, wondering why he hadn't simply told her what he was worried about. Then she took a deep breath. "It wasn't the Sigmas at all, was it?" she asked.

Tom didn't look around at the sound of her voice. There was a second of silence. "No. It wasn't the Sigmas."

Elizabeth shut the door and walked toward Tom's desk. "It was the secret society, wasn't it? You knew it all along."

He still didn't look around, but he sat back, his elbows resting on the arms of his chair. "Not all along," he answered, his voice tight as though he was measuring out his words. "I forgot about the society too at first."

"Is that why you don't want me to do the piece on racism?" Elizabeth asked, coming up to him and sitting on his desk so that he had to look at her. "Is that why you think it's so dangerous?"

His eyes met hers. Sometimes she could tell what he was thinking just by looking into those deep, dark eyes, but other times—like now—she might as well have been looking at a stone wall.

"That's exactly why," Tom answered. "Upsetting the university authorities is one thing. But this society doesn't play by the rules, Elizabeth. If you take them on, you're asking for trouble. Big trouble."

Elizabeth forced herself to remain calm. As

much as it annoyed her that Tom was treating her like a weak female, she was also touched by his concern.

"I'm not afraid of some stupid secret society," she said. "We'll work together, you and I, just like before. We can get them, Tom. I know we can."

Tom leaned forward again and began tapping keys. "Not me, Elizabeth. I have enough trouble with the dean on my case for causing a stir around here. I don't want to have anything to do with tackling the society." He glanced up at her. "And I won't run the piece, either. Assuming, that is, that you live to write it."

There were a few seconds when Elizabeth was so shocked by Tom's words that she could only gaze back at him as though he'd suddenly turned into something ugly and inappropriate for the newsroom of a television station: an earthworm, for instance. Then her calm vanished.

"I don't believe I'm hearing this!" she shouted. "I really don't! Whatever happened to the truth at any price? Whatever happened to all your principles and ideals? You mean that was just talk, Tom Watts? You mean the minute things get a little heavy, you change your mind?"

"You don't understand, Elizabeth—"

"But I do understand. I understand perfectly." She was already on her feet and halfway across the room. "You're the one who doesn't understand." Reaching the door, she wrenched it open and turned back to the room.

Tom was staring at the screen again.

"Those creeps hurt a friend of mine, Tom. Maybe they think they can do what they want because they hide behind masks and locked doors—and maybe you think they can, too—but I don't!"

She slammed the door shut behind her with a force that scared her.

Elizabeth had resolved that tonight, when she went out with William, she wouldn't talk about her work at WSVU or Tom Watts. Tonight she would stick to things that interested William. She would give all her attention to him.

After all, Tom had turned out not to be the man she'd thought he was. Maybe if she gave William more of a chance, he would turn out to be the right man for her after all.

As always, William arrived at the dorm looking as though he'd just stepped out of a Hollywood romance, his hair perfectly combed, his clothes immaculate, and a single white rose in his hand.

William complimented her on her outfit and she complimented him on his. He told her about a debate he'd had with his medieval drama professor, and she agreed that his professor was being too rigid, but didn't mention Tom; didn't mention how it reminded her of a certain other rigid person she'd encountered that day. He told her how the color of the moon had reminded him of a Japanese poem about two friends who have grown apart, but she didn't tell him about her fight with Tom.

As they strolled hand in hand across the campus Elizabeth asked William about the jazz quartet they were going to hear, and he talked knowledgeably and enthusiastically about their music and influences. Then he told her a funny story about getting his car repaired in Mexico the summer before. Elizabeth was still laughing as the waiter led them to a table in the coffeehouse.

"So what about you?" William asked once they were seated. "I've been doing all the talking so far. What have you been up to today?"

Elizabeth opened her mouth, intending to tell him about her problems with her English paper and the piece of plastic she'd found in her salad at lunch. She was going to make a joke about the plastic and not being able to find its caloric value in her dict book.

Much to her surprise, however, what she heard herself say was "I had another fight with Tom."

William's smile locked and his eyes became distant, but Elizabeth couldn't seem to stop herself.

"He absolutely refuses to let me do the

racism story, or to have anything to do with it himself, because now we're both pretty sure that the secret society is involved."

William picked up the menu and began to study it. "Secret society?" he asked as though they were talking about salad dressings. "What secret society?"

Elizabeth explained the little she knew about the society, including what she'd uncovered when she was doing the research for the hazing story.

"How can Tom be so sure this society really exists?" William asked when she finished. "It just sounds like a campus myth to me." He put the menu down. "I've certainly never heard any rumors about it. Not one."

She couldn't hide her surprise. "Really?" William knew everything that was going on at SVU, even though he remained apart from most of it. "Are you sure?"

He nodded. "Sure I'm sure."

"But I know I'm not the only one," Elizabeth said. "A lot of people I know have heard rumors, even if they're pretty vague. And things have happened . . ."

William leaned forward, thoughtful and concerned. "Can you remember who first told you about this society, Elizabeth? The Thetas? Nina? Someone in one of your classes?"

Elizabeth drew her eyebrows together, trying

to remember. "I don't really know . . ."

William put his hand over hers. "Or was it Tom?" he asked quietly.

"Tom?"

"Yes, Tom," William said. He leaned back and signaled the waiter. "For something so secret, he does seem to know a lot about it."

Underneath the table, Isabella slipped off her left shoe and rubbed her foot against her leg, trying to wake it up. She brought her soda glass to her lips so that Danny wouldn't see her yawn. Not that his conversation wasn't interesting. Danny's conversation was great. The trouble was that they'd been sitting in Pizza Paradiso for over an hour and a half, waiting for Tom, and had just about run out of superficial, meaningless things to say. She'd be telling him the story of her life soon if Tom didn't show up.

At least I can't complain that Tom Watts is like every other guy I know, Isabella thought. Every other guy she knew would give his meal card for the chance of going out with her. Tom, on the other hand, not only didn't seem to know that Isabella was alive, even when he was being tricked into going out with her he didn't turn up.

Isabella leaned across the table and grabbed Danny's wrist. "What time is it?" she demanded. "Is it time for breakfast yet?"

Danny laughed. "I don't think it's quite that late, Izzy." He looked toward the door for at least the tenth time in the last hour. "But it's definitely way past dinnertime."

"Tell me about it." Isabella groaned. "My stomach thinks my mouth's gone into retirement." She picked up the menu. "We have to order, Danny, or I'll be the first person in the history of SVU to be fed pizza intravenously."

"Five more minutes," Danny begged. "If Tom doesn't show in five more minutes, we'll order."

Isabella frowned. "Five minutes? You promise?"

Danny nodded. "When he didn't show at the gym, I left notes for him everywhere. He'll come, I know he will."

It's amazing, Isabella told herself as she sat back to wait five more minutes for the elusive Tom Watts. *I haven't been on one date with Tom yet and already my love's being put to the test.* The question was, Did she care enough to wait for him to show up before she ate, or would she rather eat without him? Isabella's stomach rumbled. She'd rather eat without him, that was the answer. She looked over at Danny, who, besides giving up his own time to help her out, had spent hours patiently talking to her about Tom and was doing his best to get them together.

"All right," Isabella reluctantly agreed. "But

not six minutes or seven minutes, you understand? No more than five."

The seductive aroma of tomato sauce seasoned with oregano and basil wafted through the restaurant and Isabella's eye idly ran down the list of pizzas: anchovy and black olive; broccoli and pine nuts; goat's cheese and sun-dried tomatoes.

"Oh my gosh!" she cried suddenly, picking up the menu and waving it in front of Danny's face. "Look at this! They have pineapple pizza!"

Danny stared back at her as though she'd just said something astounding. "Pineapple pizza?" he asked. "*You* like pineapple pizza?"

Isabella nodded. "I know it's not the purist's choice, but I'm crazy about it." She closed her eyes, imagining taking her first bite. She could practically taste the juicy sweetness of the fruit and the spicy heat of the sauce. "There's something about the combination of pineapple and tomatoes that I find very satisfying," she confided. She opened her eyes again. Danny was still staring at her. "The only pizza I like better is avocado, red onion, and black bean."

"Avocado, red onion, and black bean?" Danny rolled his eyes like a man being driven mad. "Where do you get pizza like that around here?"

She stared back at him as though he'd just confessed that he didn't know where to get water. "You mean you've never been to Julio's?" she asked. "Out by the shore?"

Danny shook his head. "I've never even heard of it."

She patted his hand. "You have led a deprived life, my friend. You haven't even begun to live until you've had one of Julio's pizzas."

Both of them looked at Danny's watch.

"How far away did you say it was?" he asked, his eyes following the minute hand.

Isabella slid her shoe back on. "We could call in our order and be there as they're taking it out of the oven."

Danny's eyes met hers. "What about Tom?"

"You can bring him back a slice if there's any left over," Isabella answered.

At a remote cottage, high in the hills, stretched out by the side of a star-shaped pool, Celine Boudreaux was thinking about the secret society as she watched Peter Wilbourne dive into the unnaturally blue water.

"I wonder . . ." she murmured to herself. "I really and truly do wonder . . ."

Celine had heard the rumors about the society as soon as she had arrived on campus. Among them was the identity of the society's leader. The name most whispered was of someone wealthy and powerful, someone well connected and confident, someone ruthless and uncompromising when it came to getting his own way. Someone who was exactly the sort of person Celine could admire and respect.

"Peter," Celine whispered. "Peter Wilbourne the Third."

A cool spray of water fell over Celine as Peter reached her. "What are you looking so serious about?" he asked, leaning against the side of the pool. "You're supposed to be having a good time."

Celine smiled. "I am having a good time, sugar." She reached out and pushed a strand of hair from his forehead. "I had no idea you knew someone with a place like this. It's absolutely divine."

Laughing, Peter lifted himself from the water and settled against Celine's lounge chair. "I know everyone," he informed her without any undue modesty. "You want to do a little traveling? I can get us a house in the mountains of Spain. Or a sailboat on the Riviera, or a town house in London, or a ranch in Argentina." He lightly ran his hand along her arm. "You name it, baby, and I know someone who will get it for us."

"I don't suppose you have any friends in campus housing," Celine drawled. "What I'd really like is a new roommate."

"I'd like you to have a new roommate, too," Peter said. "That girl has caused me nothing but trouble since she got here."

Celine's smile looked as though it had been carved by a knife. "She does have a talent for getting in the way, doesn't she?"

"More like a genius." Peter winked. "It's lucky I do have some friends in administration or she could have caused me some real problems over the thing with Winston."

Celine gazed back, taking in this information, planning her next sentence.

"Well, the princess is on another crusade now," she said casually. She watched him through half-closed lids. "Now she's all wound up about racism on campus because of what happened to her friend."

Peter's hand stopped stroking her. "Bryan Nelson's a friend of Elizabeth's?"

"No, not him." Celine rolled over on her stomach. "The girl. Nina."

"Oh, her," Peter said, running one finger down the back of her leg. His voice was edged with caution. "But I had the impression that the attack wasn't aimed at her. It was Bryan they wanted."

Celine took in this information. It didn't take a brain as big as the Mississippi to realize that Peter knew more about the attack than he was admitting.

"That's not the way Little Miss Lois Lane sees it," Celine informed him, putting a hand over her mouth as she yawned. "Our girl reporter is taking this personally."

"You don't mean Elizabeth and Watts are

going to make that their next big story, do you?" He was trying to sound matter-of-fact, but Celine could tell that he was as casual as a haute couture model posing in swimwear.

Celine's tongue glided over her lips. "I do believe so," she said softly, glancing over her shoulder at him. "You know what crusaders they are. They just can't leave anything alone."

Peter's handsome face was as hard as stone. "Maybe this time they'll have to," he said.

Tom was so upset about his argument with Elizabeth that he completely forgot about going to the gym with Danny. Instead, he threw himself into his work, refusing even to answer the phone. It wasn't until he was finally leaving WSVU for the day that he played the answering machine and heard Danny's message about getting together at Pizza Paradiso if he didn't show up for their workout.

"I could use a little male companionship," Tom told himself as he left the studio. "Maybe a pizza with Danny will take my mind off my troubles."

He was just about to start across the quad when he saw one of his troubles pass by. It was the beautiful blond trouble named Elizabeth, and she was holding William White's hand and listening to him with rapt attention.

Tom caught his breath. The sight of

Elizabeth and William together always hit him like a harpoon in the heart, not simply because it wasn't Tom walking with Elizabeth and holding her hand. It was because she and William looked so perfect together. They were both golden and striking, but William's icy arrogance and Elizabeth's warm vivacity set each other off.

"A match made in heaven," Tom muttered as they glided by, oblivious to anyone but themselves. Only, for him it was more like a match made in hell. He couldn't even ask himself what Elizabeth saw in William. It was obvious what she saw.

Tom watched them disappear down the path. He'd stopped counting the number of times he'd wanted to warn Elizabeth against her new boyfriend. What could he say? *I just have this feeling? I never really liked him? He's too good to be true? Haven't you ever read* The Portrait of Dorian Gray?

All thoughts of Danny and pizza forgotten, Tom shoved his hands into his pockets and headed back to the dorm. Though Tom had never heard anyone say anything against William White, he just didn't like him. There was something he didn't trust about those smooth good looks and immaculate manners. Something that gave him the creeps.

Not that he could say anything now, of course. Elizabeth hadn't disguised the fact that she was disappointed in Tom. If he said anything now, she'd only think it was sour grapes on his part.

Tom entered the room he shared with Danny and locked the door behind him. He stood for a second, just listening, then went over and pulled the curtains closed. Moving as stealthily as a thief or a spy, as stealthily as a man with a secret, Tom opened his closet and took down a small metal chest hidden at the back of the top shelf. He sat on the bed and unlocked the chest with a key that he wore on a chain around his neck.

Tom removed several papers and stacks of photographs, a china rabbit, a worn man's wallet, and a silver charm bracelet from the box. At the very bottom was a wad of cotton. Tom unwrapped it slowly. "If Elizabeth's disappointed in me now, she should see this," he whispered.

Held in the flat of Tom's palm was a silver ring, shaped like a broken star.

Chapter Four

Last night Jessica lay beneath an enormous desert sky with Mike's arms around her, watching for shooting stars while he talked about their future. Then, Jessica had wanted to stand on the highest mesa and shout out her love. "I love Mike McAllery!" she'd wanted to scream. "Forever and ever!" Last night, she wouldn't have cared who heard her—not even if their names were Ned and Alice Wakefield.

Today, however, Jessica was feeling different. As the lowrider pulled into the parking lot of their apartment building, Jessica wasn't quite as sure of herself as she'd been the day before, hundreds of miles from the campus and her friends. Last night, sleeping in the desert, she and Mike had been in a world of their own. Now they were back in the real world with everyone else.

His timing perfect, Steven Wakefield emerged from the building as Mike and Jessica climbed off the bike. The sight of her brother made Jessica's heart drop like a popped balloon. Suddenly she remembered a couple of things she'd forgotten in the excitement of the elopement. One of those things was that she'd missed two days of classes and yesterday's shift at the coffeehouse.

"Hey, there's Steven," Mike said, slipping his arm around Jessica's shoulders. He kissed the top of her head. "Maybe we should go over and say hello."

Another of those things was that she was going to have to tell her family and friends that she was married. It wasn't the kind of thing you could forget to mention. Somehow, standing on top of a mesa proclaiming her love and telephoning Mr. and Mrs. Wakefield to tell them she'd married a man they wouldn't approve of weren't the same thing. Jessica wasn't sure she was ready for this; not right now. Without thinking about it, she slipped her left hand, the one wearing Mike's ring, into the pocket of her jacket.

"Okay," Jessica said brightly. "Let's say hi."

Steven had stopped at the bottom of the stairs and was scowling at them with his usual disapproval.

Jessica forced herself to smile. "Morning, Steven."

"Morning?" Steven's eyes went to the sleeping bags and the overnight satchel they were carrying. "This is your idea of morning?" He turned to Jessica. "Why aren't you in school?" he demanded. "Where have you been?"

Jessica stared back at her brother, but it was her father she was seeing. Her father was angry. Her father was going to be even angrier when he found out what she'd done. Beside her, Mike shifted. *He's waiting for me to tell Steven,* Jessica thought as a wave of panic threatened to drown her. Suddenly she was sure. She wasn't ready to tell Steven about the marriage. Not like this, standing in the parking lot with sand and dead insects embedded in her clothes. Not when he was almost sure to go straight to the nearest phone to tell their parents.

"What makes you think it's any of your business?" Jessica snapped, wanting nothing more than to be safe inside her own apartment. "You're not my mother."

"Jessica—" Mike began.

"No, I'm your brother!" Steven shouted back. "And I have a right—"

"Just a minute, *brother,*" Mike cut in. "I happen to have a few rights here myself."

Steven turned on him, his face the picture of intense, almost painful dislike. "Talking to me is not one of them," Steven said. "I wouldn't waste my breath talking to trash like you."

Mike took a step forward. "Really? Is that what

81

you think I am, you uptight android? Trash?"

"I don't think it," Steven shot back. "I *know* it."

"Tell him," Mike said. He looked at Jessica. "Tell Mr. Wonderful here what I am."

Jessica looked from Mike to Steven. Both of them were staring at her, waiting. Another wave of panic broke over her head. If she told Steven now, he'd be on the phone to her parents before she unpacked her overnight bag and they'd be on her doorstep before she could move. Somehow, that wasn't what she'd planned.

"Stop it!" Jessica yelled, tears beginning to trickle down her cheeks. "Both of you, stop it. I can't stand any more of this!"

Mike reached for her. "Jess, I just—"

She broke away from him and ran past them, through the door of the building and up the stairs, Mike at her heels.

As soon as they were in their apartment he dropped the sleeping bags in the hall and took her in his arms. "What's wrong?" he asked. "Why didn't you tell Steven we're married? Why didn't you tell him I'm your husband?"

Jessica looked into those golden eyes. She couldn't say it was because she didn't want Steven to know—it would hurt Mike too much.

"He was shouting at me," she said, more tears filling her eyes. "I didn't want to tell him when he was shouting." She pressed against him, listening to his heart. "Besides," she whispered, "it's our honeymoon. If I told Steven, my parents would be down here by dinnertime. I want it just to be us for a couple of days. I want it to be perfect."

Mike hugged her tight. "But you are going to tell him," he insisted. "And them."

"Of course I am," Jessica said. She didn't say when.

Tom stepped into the room and froze. His eyes moved from one side to the other. As far as he could see, everything was exactly as he and Danny had left it that morning. His pajama bottoms were draped over the back of his chair. Danny's free weights were lying on his bed. The pizza box Danny had brought back for him last night was still on the dresser.

"Something's not right," Tom muttered. He didn't know how he knew, but he was sure that someone had been in the room while he and Danny were out. It was as if he could smell it.

He slipped his keys into his pocket as he walked over to his desk. If someone had gotten in, it wouldn't be because of Danny. Nothing on his desk had been touched. Looking uneasy, Tom opened the top side drawer, but all it contained were the things it should contain. He opened the second drawer and then the third, but they, too, were just as they should be.

"Maybe I'm just imagining it," Tom told

himself. "Maybe I'm more stressed out than I thought."

His hand reached forward and pulled out the middle drawer. On top of the lined yellow pad he used for notes was a plain white envelope. Tom was so unsurprised that he didn't even blink. He glanced at the clock, checking the time to make sure that Danny wasn't likely to come back unexpectedly. Then he sat down at the desk and opened the envelope.

Inside was a single sheet of white paper. The message on it was made from words cut from magazines. It was only one line, but Tom lost track of the time as he sat reading it over and over, trying to decide what he should do.

"I don't have any choice," he finally admitted. "I'll have to show Elizabeth. There's no other way to stop her."

Suddenly the door opened behind him. "What are you doing sitting in the dark?" Danny asked. "Has our room had its own private blackout?"

Tom jumped up, stuffing the note back into its envelope and into the drawer. "No, I just got lost in my thoughts, that's all."

Danny switched on the light. "You mean like last night?" he asked. "What are you trying to do, Tombo? Figure out the meaning of life?"

Tom laughed, hoping he sounded happier than he felt. "No, just the usual. You know, sorting out the TV station and stuff."

Danny threw his books on his own desk. "I've said it before and I'll say it again—you work too hard." He smacked Tom on the shoulder. "How about taking a little break tonight? We could ride out to the beach on our bikes. We haven't done that in ages."

Tom was about to say no, but then he thought better of it. Danny was beginning to get suspicious about the way he was behaving. The last thing Tom needed was to have Danny on his case, too.

"Okay," he said, "I'll race you out there. Loser buys the hot fries in that café out by Pirate's Point."

Danny slapped him on the back. "Deal."

Nina leaned against the nurses' station with a sigh. Her mother was saying good-bye to everyone for her, which meant that Nina didn't have to say anything. All she had to do was be ready to smile and nod should anyone actually look her way. It was funny how little time it had taken Nina to forget how her mother always took control. After only a few weeks at college, Nina had really gotten used to the idea that she was the person running her life.

While Grace Harper and the head nurse discussed the aftereffects of shock, Nina looked over the desk. The room roster lay open beside the telephone. Her mother blamed Bryan for what had happened and had forbidden her to speak to him, but Nina found her eyes moving automatically down the list, searching for his name.

There it was: *Nelson, Bryan, Room 46, Ward K*. Nina glanced behind her. Ward K was just through the swinging doors and across the corridor. She turned back to her mother and Nurse Zahn. They were still deep in conversation.

Do it, Nina urged herself. *You can't leave here without at least saying good-bye.*

Slowly and quietly, she started moving backward, not taking her eyes from her mother. When she reached the doors, she took a deep breath and hurled herself through them, expecting to hear Grace Harper's clear, authoritative voice calling after her, "Where are you going, sweetheart?" but all she heard was the pounding of her own heart.

Bryan was in a private room at the end of the hall. The blinds were drawn and he was lying still, his eyes closed. She couldn't tell if he was listening to the blues station that was playing softly on the radio or sleeping.

"Bryan?" Nina whispered.

His eyes opened immediately. Despite the bandages covering most of his body and the bruises covering the parts of his body not covered by the bandages, his smile was as strong and bright as ever. "Don't tell me," he said. "You've come to say you never want to go out with me again. But you should think about it, Nina. The first date's always the worst."

Nina laughed, shutting the door behind her and going over to sit by his bed. "Oh, I don't know if it was as bad as all that," she said, suddenly realizing how glad she was to see him. "At least it wasn't dull."

"Wait'll you see what happens on our third date," Bryan teased. "We get kidnapped and dropped onto the desert from a helicopter."

"Sounds like fun," Nina said. She started straightening out the get-well cards on his table. "It's too bad I won't be here for it."

Bryan touched her with his fingertips. "What do you mean, you won't be here? Where are you going?"

"Home," Nina said, still fussing with the cards. "My mother is here now. She thinks it would be better if I went back."

His touch became heavier. "I'd say, Better than what, being beaten up again? but I have the feeling that's not what we're talking about."

Nina nodded. It was unnerving how well he knew her already. "Better than waiting to transfer at the end of the semester." She forced herself to meet his eyes. "That's what I wanted to do," she admitted. "Wait till the break. But my mom thinks I should leave right away."

"You don't mean leave," Bryan said coldly. "You mean run."

"I'm scared, Bryan," she said, in almost a whisper. "I can't help it. I'm really scared."

His fingers tightened around her wrist. "Do you think I'm not, Nina? Do you think getting beaten up is my idea of a pleasant way to end an evening? I wanted to kiss you good night, not put you in the hospital."

She looked down at the cast on his leg. It was covered with writing. "I don't think of you as the type to be afraid. You're so strong—so committed."

"No, I'm not," Bryan said. "I'm just stubborn. I'm not going to give in to bullies. If you give in to people like that, they'll run everything."

"I guess I'm not much of a crusader. I just want a normal life."

"And I want everyone to have a 'normal' life," Bryan answered. "Especially the people who don't have much of a chance to fight for it themselves."

Right in the middle of the cast someone had written in black Magic Marker: DON'T LET IGNORANCE GET YOU DOWN. "Who wrote that?" asked Nina. "One of the BSU people?"

Bryan shook his head. "My dad wrote it while I was still unconscious. He wanted me to see something positive when I came around."

Nina ran her finger along the message. She couldn't help thinking that if it had been her and her mother had written something positive for her to see when she regained consciousness, it would probably have been TAKE THE MONEY AND RUN.

"So is this going to be the only visit I get from you?" Bryan asked. "Should I be taking a picture to remember you by?"

It was hard for Nina to look at Bryan and not smile. "No," she said. "I'll stop by every day." *Just as long as my mother doesn't find out,* she added to herself.

"Double hot fries, Wyatt," Tom said as they locked their bikes outside the Jolly Roger Café. "*And* a mega-large iced tea."

"All right, all right," Danny said, laughing. "But I still say I would've beaten you if it wasn't for that mini-mountain you insisted on coming up. You know I'm not good with heights."

Tom clapped him on the shoulder. "You don't have to make excuses to me, Daniel. I'm your best friend." They started down the wooden boardwalk that led to the café. "You can admit it—you're just not as good a cyclist as I am." He held the door open and waved Danny through.

Danny took a few steps into the room and then stopped so abruptly that Tom walked into him. "What a coincidence!" cried Danny. "Look who's here!"

Unreliable as ever, and forgetting that Elizabeth wasn't really speaking to Tom at the moment, Tom's heart did a movement something like a back handspring. *Elizabeth!* he thought. *It's Elizabeth!*

But it wasn't.

"It's Isabella!"

Tom followed Danny's gaze: It was true, Isabella Ricci was sitting at a corner table by herself. With her dark, flowing hair and her designer slacks and blouse, she looked out of place in the fishing net and driftwood decor of the Jolly Roger. What was it with this girl? Tom wondered. Every time he turned around lately, he bumped into her.

"I'll get us a table while you go say hello," Tom said quickly.

"What are you talking about? We can't let Isabella sit all by herself." Danny grabbed his arm and started hauling him across the room. "Izzy!" he called. "Mind if we join you?"

"Danny!" Tom hissed, trying to yank him back. It wasn't that he disliked Isabella, but she wasn't his type. She was all right for someone whose clothes all had names like Guess? and Rampage, but he didn't really have anything to say to her. After a threatening letter and a tenmile bike ride, Tom wanted to chill, not engage in forced conversation while he worried about smelling like low tide.

But Danny was already pulling out two chairs and motioning Tom to sit down.

"What do you know," Danny said. "Isabella drove down here in her Land-Rover. She'll be able to give us and the bikes a ride back."

Tom stared at his friend in disbelief. One of the reasons he'd agreed to come tonight was that he'd thought hanging out with Danny really would relax him a little. He was having such a bad time at the moment that some easy companionship had seemed like a good idea. The sophisticated Isabella Ricci and her talk of sororities, shopping, and social events did not come under the category of "easy companionship." She was the sort of girl Tom would have hung out with in the old days, when he was a football hero and one of the biggest men on campus, with nothing on his mind but his own ego. But besides that, being with a girl he didn't want to be with was only going to remind him more of the girl he did want to be with. It wasn't Isabella's fault that she wasn't Elizabeth, of course, but it wasn't Tom's fault either.

"I can't stay," Tom said. "I'm sorry, Danny, I just remembered something I—something I was supposed to do tonight."

Danny was too surprised to be angry. "What are you talking about?" he asked. "We just got here." He pushed a chair toward Tom. "Sit down and have your fries, and Isabella will drive us back to campus."

Tom, however, was quickly walking backward.

"I can't, Danny. Really. I have to go." He bumped into a table. "I'll see you back at the room."

"You're being stupid, man," argued Danny. "You're being—"

But Tom didn't hear what else he was besides stupid. He was already outside, trying to disentangle himself from some fishing net hanging on the porch.

Something soft and delicate brushed against Jessica's lips. Memories of their first night in their own home as husband and wife drifted through her mind. Forgetting about Steven, they'd spent most of the evening making love. Marriage, Jessica had decided by the time she and Mike were eating grilled cheese sandwiches and sharing a bottle of beer by candlelight, had a lot to recommend it.

That same something brushed Jessica's lips once more. Slowly, she opened her eyes. Mike's mouth touched hers again. "Good morning, Mrs. McAllery," he said. "And how are you on this beautiful morning?"

Jessica stretched against his body, closing her arms around his warm, smooth skin. "I'm just wonderful, Mr. McAllery," she said between kisses. "I'm just as wonderful as I could possibly be."

"You are that," he breathed. "You are the most wonderful thing in the world."

Over his shoulder, her eye caught sight of the

clock radio. "I'm also late," she said, gently pulling out of their embrace. "I've got a nine o'clock class I can't afford to cut again."

Much to Jessica's surprise, he didn't argue. "Far be it from me to cause you to miss one minute of school," Mike said, sitting up. He grinned. "Anyway, I know you're anxious to see your friends so you can tell them the news."

Jessica grinned back. It was true, she was excited about telling her friends. They weren't going to believe that she was no longer Jessica Wakefield, just another teenage freshman, but Mrs. Michael McAllery, a married woman.

"I can't wait to see the look on Isabella's face when I tell her," she admitted.

"It's the look on your brother's face when he finds out that I want to see," Mike said.

Elizabeth reread the paper she was holding in her hand. It wasn't a long message, but it was a chilling one nonetheless. *Stop her*, it said. *Or we will*. Trying not to show how upset she was by the clumsily cut-out and glued-on letters, she looked up at Tom. "So?" she asked. "What does this have to do with me?"

"You know what it has to do with you," he answered. "*Her* is you."

Elizabeth pulled on the end of a strand of hair. "I don't see how you can be so sure of that," she said bravely. "It could be anyone."

"But it isn't anyone," Tom said. "See the broken star printed at the bottom? I told you, this is from the secret society. Somehow, they found out about your—our—interest in them, and they're warning us off."

Elizabeth handed him back the note. Up until a few minutes ago, she hadn't believed that people received threats like this. Not people like her, at any rate. She also hadn't believed that the secret society was quite as sinister or as serious as Tom had tried to tell her it was.

"Well, what do we do now?" she asked.

Tom stared at her as though she were a brick wall and he'd just run into her. "What do you mean, *what do we do now*? What have I been trying to tell you all along, Elizabeth? We do nothing, that's what we do." He put the sheet of paper back in its envelope and into the pocket of his jacket. "That's why I showed it to you. So you'd understand why I was being so stubborn about not doing the story."

As frightened as Elizabeth was, she was also determined. "You don't mean you're going to let this stop us, do you?" she asked.

Tom put his hands on her shoulders. She wasn't sure if he wanted to hold her down or shake her. "Elizabeth," he said slowly, "you and I are not Lois Lane and Clark Kent. Bullets will go through me and I can't scoop you up in my arms and fly you to safety when things get rough. These guys mean business, Elizabeth. If we go on with this, we're not going to write the next big story, we're going to *be* the next story: *WSVU Reporters Killed in Tragic Accident.*"

Elizabeth steadied her pounding heart, her brain working fast. As a reporter, she'd always believed that if there was a problem, there also had to be a solution. The problem here was that she and Tom might be seriously hurt if they pursued the story. So what was the solution?

"Not necessarily," she answered at last.

He raised one eyebrow. "Not necessarily? How are you planning to avoid that?"

The words came out by themselves. "By secretly finding out who the head of the secret society is. If we expose him, the whole organization will fall apart."

Tom looked thoughtful. "Maybe." He bit his lip. "Maybe," he said again. "But I'm still not sure it's worth the risk."

It seemed like such an obvious and perfect solution to Elizabeth that she couldn't help feeling impatient with Tom again. Was this nervous, backtracking Tom Watts the real Tom Watts, or was something going on that he hadn't told her?

"I don't know what risk you mean," she said shortly. "If we're careful, they'll never know."

"They knew we were thinking about doing something," Tom reasoned. "They knew we'd made a connection between them and what happened to Nina. Why shouldn't they know we're trying to discover who their leader is?"

It was Elizabeth who looked thoughtful now. Tom had a point. How had the secret society known that they'd found out anything about them? How had they known about Elizabeth's planned report? She leaned back, folding her arms. "That's a good question," she said. She made a face. "I wish I had a good answer."

Tom sighed. "Well, until you do, I think we'd better put this idea on hold, don't you?"

Elizabeth shook her head. "No," she said. "I think we should just put that on the list of things we need to find out."

Jessica was in a great mood as she strode across campus, her books hugged against her chest and her hair blowing in a warm breeze. She smiled as she passed the other students, laughing and chatting as they hurried to their classes. It felt as though she'd been away for weeks, not days, but it was good to be back; good to be part of it all.

She turned left, quickening her pace as she spotted Isabella, Denise Waters, and several of their Theta sisters talking together at the steps of the science building. Ever since the Thetas dumped her from their sorority, Jessica had tried to avoid them, but today she didn't care. Magda Helperin and Alison Quinn, the president and vice president of the Thetas, might not like Michael McAllery, but everybody else would be green with envy when they found out that he and Jessica were married.

No one stopped talking or even looked at her as Jessica attached herself to the group. Alison was talking about what she was wearing to some big party they were having that weekend, and everyone else was pretending to be nailed to the ground with interest.

"Hi," Jessica said.

Isabella looked over and smiled, but the girl beside Jessica, a skinny redhead with too many freckles, said, "Shhh."

Jessica waited for Alison to finish describing the sleeves of her new dress. Jessica hadn't bought any new clothes in weeks, not since she realized she had overdrawn her allowance for the rest of the semester and had had to start working as a waitress at the coffeehouse. She'd barely made enough to buy a new pair of socks, never mind a dress.

"Gosh, I haven't seen you guys in a while," Jessica said when Alison was finally done.

But Alison, apparently, wasn't done; she'd only been taking a breather. "What's this I hear about you?" Alison asked, turning to Denise. "Someone said they saw you playing pool with a guy. I thought most of the guys on this campus bored you to tears."

Denise gave Alison a Mona Lisa smile. "Now, who told you that?" she asked. "It couldn't have been Bettina Wainwright, could it?" Denise turned to the rest of the group. "Bettina was there with Bruce Patman!"

"Bruce Patman!" Alison echoed, distracted from Denise and her date. "But that's impossible. Bettina's been going out with Louie Elafi for ages. I saw them mooning all over each other at the movies last night."

Denise shrugged. "Maybe I was wrong," she said. "Maybe it was Louie, but I mistook him for Bruce. You know what the light in the pool hall is like."

Jessica decided to try to catch their attention another way. "I went out with Bruce Patman in high school," she announced.

"Did I tell you Tony got tickets to see The Freeze-Drieds Saturday night?" asked Kimberly Schyler, her voice so unattractively loud that it drowned out Jessica.

Jessica had never heard of The Freeze-Drieds, but everyone else had. They started screeching as if Kimberly had said Elvis Presley had come back to life and was doing a private performance just for her.

"I have some news, too," Jessica nearly shouted when the screeching had died down.

"Really?" Isabella asked. "What is it, Jess?"

Alison decided to act as though Jessica

hadn't spoken at all. "Did you hear about the big dance the Interfraternity Council is planning for Parents' Weekend?" she asked. "It's going to have a sixties theme."

Only half-listening, Jessica bit her lip, waiting for another nanosecond of silence in which to tell her news.

"That's cool," Kimberly said. "You won't be able to get my parents off the dance floor. One Beatles song and they start acting like they're fifteen."

The group started walking toward the door of the building.

"Mine too," the redhead said. "It's sooo embarrassing. If I tell my mom it's going to be a six-ties night, she'll probably show up in hiphuggers."

Denise groaned. "That's nothing. My folks will jump at the chance to drag their love beads out of the attic."

Isabella came up beside Jessica. "What about your parents?" she asked.

Jessica didn't want to talk about her parents any more than she wanted to talk about Alison's wardrobe or The Freeze-Drieds. She wanted to talk about her husband. "My parents hate the Beatles," she snapped.

Isabella gave her a look. "I didn't mean that," she said. "I meant are they coming for Parents' Weekend?"

Suddenly the significance of the conversation

hit Jessica. It was a lot like being hit by a truck. In all the excitement and trauma of marrying Mike, she'd completely forgotten about Parents' Weekend. Her mother still talked about her four years at SVU as some of the best years of her life. The only thing that would keep her away was a broken neck. Jessica had been planning to wait for just the right moment to tell them about Mike. The right moment was not going to be while they were milling around with hundreds of other parents, comparing notes on how their children were doing.

Jessica swallowed hard. "Well, yes," she said. "I guess they are."

"You mean you haven't thought about what you're going to do?" Isabella asked, not hiding her surprise.

Jessica shrugged. "Not really. I've had other things on my mind. Mike and I—"

"Forget about Mike and you," Isabella said. She opened the door to her astronomy classroom and marched in. "You'd better figure out what you're going to do while your parents are here." She looked over her shoulder. "If you want, you can move back in with me, you know."

"Move back in?"

"Till they're gone, I mean," Isabella said. She sat down.

For the first time in days, Jessica stopped thinking about Mike. "That's great!" She leaned down and gave her old roommate a hug. "Izzy, that's really great." That meant she wouldn't be forced into telling Mr. and Mrs. Wakefield the truth before she was ready; before she had everything worked out. She hugged Isabella again. "You're a great friend!"

Isabella gave her a rueful smile. "I sure hope you have the chance to return the favor some-day," she said.

Chapter Five

Jessica hummed to herself as she fixed Mike's breakfast. She hadn't told him about Isabella's suggestion that she move back into the dorm while Mr. and Mrs. Wakefield were on campus, but she was beginning to think it was one of the best ideas Isabella had ever had.

Jessica measured out the coffee precisely. Too much and he complained that he couldn't work because his nerves were jangled. Too little and he complained that he might as well be drinking water.

Isabella had never complained about her coffee. Jessica sighed. The truth was that the more she thought about going back to the dorm for a day or two, the more she realized how much she wanted to. She missed the nights she and Isabella used to sit up till all hours, eating junk food and talking about guys. She missed the

Saturday afternoons spent shopping. Maybe it wouldn't be so bad if she could talk to her best friend from high school, the Countess di Mondicci, who used to be called Lila Fowler. Lila was a married woman, too, now. Lila must know what it was like; not just the wonderful parts, but the dull parts as well. But she couldn't talk to Lila—Lila was still in Italy.

Jessica started juicing oranges. She'd been a little surprised to discover that the can wasn't the natural container for orange juice. Mike insisted that people in Alaska might have to drink orange juice from concentrate, but that people in California did not. While she pressed the oranges through the juicer, her mind replayed the conversation outside the science building over and over.

Those girls might still be kids, but they were kids who were having a good time. They didn't have any worries or responsibilities. For them, life was part party, part shopping spree—just as it used to be for Jessica. Now Jessica couldn't do anything or go anywhere without first thinking about how Mike would react. Would he get mad? Would he be jealous? Would there be a fight?

"How's my favorite wife this morning?" Mike asked, coming up behind her. He wrapped his arms around her and gave her a kiss.

She kissed him back. "I'm wonderful," she said. "What about my favorite husband, how's he?"

"Wonderful." He took the glass of juice she handed him and sat at the counter. "I'm starting on that '53 Buick I told you about today. It should be fun."

Jessica set out the toast and the coffee. *He's in a good mood,* she told herself. *Now's the time to bring up Parents' Weekend.*

She slipped onto the stool beside his. "Did I tell you I ran into Isabella yesterday?" she asked casually.

Mike smiled. "What'd she think about your news?"

"My news?"

He grabbed her left hand and held it up in front of her so she could see the silver-and-turquoise ring. "Yeah, your news."

"Oh, my *news!*"

He let go of her. "You mean you didn't tell her?" His voice was instantly full of hurt.

"I tried to, Mike. I really did. But she was with a bunch of the other girls and all they wanted to talk about was parties and clothes and stuff like that. I couldn't get a word in without a crowbar."

Mike picked up his coffee. "You're lucky to be away from those snobs," he said.

"Oh, I know," Jessica answered quickly. "I know I am." She cleared her throat. "But Isabella did say that it would be okay with her if I moved back in with her for a day or two. You know, just while my folks are here."

"Move back to the dorm?" Coffee sloshed over the table as he slammed down his cup. "Why would you want to do a thing like that?"

Jessica bit her lip. "Well, I just thought that . . . you know, that it would give me a chance to break the news to my parents gently."

He shoved his cup out of his way. "For two cents I'd call them myself right now and tell them," Mike said angrily. "The only reason I haven't is that since they don't even know I exist, the person to tell them should be you."

"But I am going to tell them!" She made a move to touch him, but he pulled away. "I am, Mike, you know I am. I just want to wait for the right moment."

He got up so quickly he knocked over the stool. "The right moment to tell them was after the ceremony, Jess. That's when the right moment was." Instead of righting the stool, he shoved it out of his way, sending it crashing into the cabinets.

"Mike!"

"What's the problem?" he shouted. "Are you ashamed of me or something, Jess? Don't you think I'm good enough for you? Are your parents going to be disappointed because instead of marrying a prince you married a mechanic, is that what it is?"

He stormed from the room, Jessica running behind him.

"It's not that, Mike! You know it's nothing like that," she sobbed. "It's just that I want to tell them in person, not over the phone."

"Oh, yeah?" She flinched as he yanked his jacket from the hook in the hallway so violently that the hook flew out of the wall. "And when is that going to be, Jess? Thanksgiving? Christmas? Next Easter?"

"No!" she wailed. "It'll be soon, Mike. I swear it will. And I want you to be with me. I want them to meet you."

Mike stopped with his hand on the front door. "Then it really better be soon, Jess, because if it isn't, you're not going to know where to find me."

"I can't eat this," Mark Gathers said, pushing his plate of pancakes away untouched. "Everything tastes like wood shavings."

Enid, sitting beside Mark, continued spreading jelly on her toast. It was better to say nothing. If she opened her mouth, he'd only snap at her.

"You have to eat something," Todd said. He smiled. "The way things are going, we're going to need all the strength we can get."

Enid flinched. Maybe Todd thought that was funny, but she didn't. She was already exhausted, and the investigation had only begun.

Mark didn't think it was funny either. "Who are you kidding?" he asked. "I could live on spinach for the next couple of weeks and it wouldn't help me. You'll probably get off with a reprimand, but I'm dead meat, Todd, and you know it."

"No, I don't," Todd said staunchly. "You'll be all right, Mark. We all took some things for granted—we didn't pay enough attention, that's all. They're not going to burn us for that."

Enid fought back the disloyal thought that you really had to not be paying attention in a big way not to notice things like free vacations and a brand-new Explorer.

Mark threw his napkin into his half-empty juice glass. "Yeah, well, no one wants to hear about that now, Todd. They're not interested in our side of things. They just want us to pay."

At last Enid could say something Mark wouldn't yell at her for. "We all know who you have to thank for that," she said.

"Speak of the devil," Mark muttered. "Or should I say speak of the witch?"

Enid and Todd looked up. Elizabeth and Winston were coming toward them.

Seeing them, Winston waved. "Hi, Todd! Hi, Alex . . . Hey, Mark."

"Winston," Todd said. "How's it going?" Mark and Enid waved back.

Elizabeth smiled. "Hi!" she called.

As though they were puppets controlled by one string, Enid, Todd, and Mark all stared at her for a second in silence, and then they looked away.

"This is Elizabeth, Mom," Nina said. "Remember I told you about her?"

Nina's mother smiled politely. "You're the one who's on a diet, right?"

"Mom!" Nina rolled her eyes. "Elizabeth is the reporter for the campus TV station."

"I'm also on a diet," Elizabeth said. She extended her hand, a little surprised by the firmness of Grace Harper's grip. Somehow she wasn't what Elizabeth had been expecting. Despite the little Nina had said about her mother, Elizabeth had expected her to be charming and funny like her daughter. But Grace Harper was reserved, and if she had a sense of humor, she was keeping it a well-guarded secret. "It's nice to meet you," Elizabeth added lamely.

Mrs. Harper did not reply that it was nice to meet Elizabeth. "Reporter?" she said instead. "You're not doing a piece on what happened to Nina, are you?"

Reasoning that Nina and her mother were two people she could easily cross off her list of possible suspects as head of the secret society, Elizabeth opened her mouth to say yes, but Mrs. Harper didn't give her the chance.

"Because if that's what you're planning, you can forget it right now," Grace Harper informed her. "Nina's been through enough without you stirring things up."

Nina glanced nervously from Elizabeth to her mother. "Mom, please . . . Elizabeth dropped by to see how I was. She's my friend."

"She's a reporter," Nina's mother said. "Reporters don't have friends. Reporters don't care who gets hurt so long as they get their story."

The looks on the faces of Todd and Alexandra in the cafeteria that morning flashed through Elizabeth's mind. There were two people who would agree with Mrs. Harper. Elizabeth shoved the memory away.

"That's not true," Elizabeth protested. "I care a lot about Nina. That's why I want to find out who did this to her. I want the men responsible brought to justice."

"And I want my daughter as far away from here as she can get," Grace Harper said. "I want her to have a nice, safe life . . ."

Elizabeth raised her chin, her blue-green eyes flashing like the ocean under a hot sun. "I want everyone to have a nice, safe life," she replied.

Nina caught her breath. "That's just what Bryan said," she murmured.

Her mother heard her, too. "He's another troublemaker we won't be having anything to do with," she said. She put her arm around Nina's shoulders. "I would never have let you come here if I'd known the sort of friends you were going to make. Reporters . . . radicals . . ." She sighed. "Isn't there anyone on this campus who wants to be an accountant?"

"I guess I'll be going now," Elizabeth said to Nina. "I'm sure you and your mother want to talk, and I have a lot of work to do." She nodded at Grace Harper. "Nice meeting you," she said again.

For the first time since Elizabeth entered Nina's room, an almost warm look came into the older woman's eyes. "It was nice meeting you, too, Elizabeth," she said. "I hope you don't think I meant anything personal by what I said. It's just that Nina's all Mr. Harper and I have. That's why I'm taking her home with me."

Elizabeth hadn't realized Nina would be leaving so soon. She did her best to hide her surprise.

Nina walked Elizabeth to the door. "Thanks for stopping by," she said.

Elizabeth gave Nina a quick hug. "I'm glad you're feeling better. You wouldn't leave without saying good-bye, would you?"

"Of course I wouldn't." Nina followed her out into the hall. "Elizabeth," she said, lowering her voice. "I wanted to tell you something."

"What is it?" Elizabeth asked, immediately concerned.

Nina glanced uneasily over her shoulder. "It's just that I've been thinking about that night, and I'm pretty sure I did recognize one of the men. His voice. He was kicking Bryan and shouting at him."

An icy hand grabbed hold of Elizabeth's heart. "Who?" she asked.

"That's the problem," Nina said. "I don't know. I just know it was familiar. You know, that I'd heard it a few times, but it wasn't someone I know very well. Not a teacher or anyone in my classes, but someone I must come across now and then."

Elizabeth nodded. "Why are you telling me this, Nina?" she asked. "I thought you didn't want to have anything to do with my investigation."

Nina glanced over her shoulder again. "I guess something's making me change my mind," she said.

Celine lit a cigarette, put her feet up on Elizabeth's desk, and opened the notebook neatly labeled "WSVU."

"Lois Lane strikes again," Celine muttered as she read through her roommate's most recent notes. Despite what Peter Wilbourne had said, it was obvious that Elizabeth had no intention of giving up her investigation.

Celine smiled to herself as she brushed some ash from the page she was reading. "This time you may have bitten off more than you can chew, princess," she said happily.

There had been no mistaking the threat in Peter's words when he'd said that maybe this time Tom and Elizabeth would have to leave things alone. And there had been no mistaking his meaning when later he'd said that he hoped he could count on Celine's help. "Can the tide count on the moon?" Celine had countered.

Celine scanned the pages quickly, looking for something she didn't already know. "And there it is," she said under her breath as her eyes fell on the words *secret society*. "There it is . . ." She'd thought Elizabeth's suspicions were still totally fixed on the Sigmas. Elizabeth must be smarter than she seemed, if she'd worked that one out. And dumber, too, if she was actually planning to take on the secret society.

Celine jumped as she heard a sound outside the door. Hastily shutting the notebook, she shoved it under a history text. She was stubbing out her cigarette with a bored expression on her face when Elizabeth came into the room.

Elizabeth stopped in the doorway. "What are you doing at my desk?" she demanded.

Celine picked up a jar of gold nail polish from Elizabeth's makeup tray. "I'm doing my nails," she drawled. "What does it look like I'm doing?"

The door slammed shut. "It looks like you're going through my stuff."

Celine smiled to herself as she began to apply

113

the polish in long, even strokes. *They don't call you clever for nothing, do they, sugar?* she asked silently.

Elizabeth marched over and yanked her chair back. "Get away from my desk," she ordered. "How many times do I have to tell you to keep out of my things?"

"Oooh," Celine said, pretending to shudder. "Somebody's in a bad mood." She flashed Elizabeth one of her most insincere smiles as she got to her feet. "Don't tell me the princess is upset because her only friend in the world is leaving SVU."

That surprised her.

"How did you know Nina's leaving?" Elizabeth said. "Have you been fortune-telling with frog intestines again, Celine?"

Celine picked up the polish. "Everyone knows," she said sweetly. She picked up the ashtray and the cotton balls. "Like my granny always says, good news travels fast." She sat down on Elizabeth's bed.

Elizabeth blew some stray ash from her blotter. "I don't think that's very funny," she snapped. "I would have thought that even you would have a little more sympathy for someone who was the victim of a vicious, totally unprovoked attack."

Elizabeth was searching for something on her desk. *Darn*, Celine thought. *I must have put the notebook back in the wrong place.*

"Unprovoked?" Celine asked, hoping to distract her. "I know you reporters like to customize the truth, but don't you think *unprovoked* is at least a teeny exaggeration?"

Elizabeth looked up. "No," she said angrily. "I don't think so. What do you think Nina did to provoke the attack? Breathe?"

Celine carefully covered another nail with gold. "Oh, not Nina," she said. "Him. Bryan. Everybody knows that he's always stirring things up." She pointed the polish brush at the gold locket around her roommate's neck. "Long before you decided to drag the Sigmas through the mud, Bryan Nelson was accusing them of discriminating against minority students and trying to get their affiliation with the school revoked."

"And you consider that provocation?"

"Yes," Celine said smoothly. "Yes, I do." Pretending to be concentrating on her nails, she watched Elizabeth finally locate the WSVU notebook.

"And I consider this provocation," Elizabeth said heatedly. "This book was inside my desk when I left the room, not on top."

Celine didn't glance over. "Don't flatter yourself, princess. I couldn't be bothered reading your precious notes. I'm sure they're about as exciting as the instructions for my VCR."

Elizabeth jammed the notebook into her bag. "Well, you don't have to worry," she fumed. "Because you'll never get the chance to read them again."

"Drat!" A slow smile spread across Celine's face as Elizabeth slammed back out of the room and a drop of gold fell on Elizabeth's bedspread. "Now look what she made me do."

Elizabeth sat on the linen cloth William had spread over the sand, feeling a little giddy from the half a glass of wine she'd drunk. *This is perfect,* she was thinking. *This is the date I used to dream about when I was a little girl.*

Elizabeth sighed. The night was warm, and the sky was black and studded with stars. Moonlight shimmered on the ocean, and if you closed your eyes, the breaking waves sounded like mermaids singing. William had refused to tell her where they were going, driving along the coast for what seemed like hours. And then, just when Elizabeth had begun to wonder if they were driving in circles, he'd said, "We're here!" and pulled off the road. Producing bread, cheese, fruit, and wine from the trunk of the car, he'd led her to this romantic cove, tucked between the cliffs of the shore.

"*A loaf of bread, a jug of wine, and thou . . .*" William whispered, his arms suddenly around her.

Perfect, Elizabeth repeated as his lips moved closer. *The date from my fantasies . . .* She closed her eyes, her mouth to his, the sound of her heartbeat melding with the sound of the ocean.

Perfect except for one thing, a traitorous voice whispered in her ear. *It's the right night, and the right spot, and all the right things—but it's the wrong man . . .*

William's kissing became more passionate.

Afraid that she was leading him on, Elizabeth gently pulled away. "I—I—I'm sorry," she stammered. "It's just that I'm—I'm worried about the time."

"The time?" He caught his breath. "You're worried about the *time?*"

She nodded, disentangling herself from his embrace. "I've still got a lot of work to do tonight."

William's eyes were suddenly sharp as crystals. "When I asked you to go for a drive, you said you'd finished your homework," he reminded her. "You gave me the impression that you had some time for me."

"I did—I do," said Elizabeth quickly. "But it's not work for school. It's for my piece for WSVU. I still have a lot of research to do."

Looking as though he'd been carved out of alabaster, William began packing up the picnic things. "I thought Tom wasn't going to let you do the special on racism," he said coldly. "I thought you'd abandoned that idea."

Elizabeth shrugged. She'd promised herself that she wouldn't say anything more about the secret society to anybody, but William, of course, was not anybody. And he deserved some sort of explanation—even if the explanation was really only an excuse.

She shook her head. "No," said Elizabeth. "No, I haven't abandoned anything. I'm still determined to find out the truth." As briefly as she could, she explained about the note Tom had received and Nina's certainty that she recognized one of her assailants.

"The more I think about it, the more I'm convinced that Peter Wilbourne is involved," she said. "Peter's voice is one that Nina would know."

"Peter Wilbourne? Don't make me laugh." William pulled her to her feet. "You mean you think he's the head of this mythical secret society of yours? He's too in love with himself and he doesn't have the brains."

"It's not mythical," Elizabeth protested. "I told you, William, Tom received a threatening note."

He gave her a look. "You have only Tom's word for that," William said.

Elizabeth watched as he folded up the tablecloth. "What are you suggesting?" she demanded.

"I'm not suggesting anything." He slipped a hand under her elbow. "I'm suggesting that we stop for gas on the way back or you won't be able to work tonight because we'll be walking home."

*   *   *

Nothing was all bad, Jessica reflected as she and Mike left the diner. Even a major fight and half a day of tears and heartbreak had its good side: the making up. As part of the making up for this morning's fight, Mike had brought her back to the place where he'd first proposed. A cheese omelette, home fries, and a candle stuck in an empty beer bottle might not be everyone's idea of a romantic dinner for two, but as far as Jessica was concerned sipping champagne at a café on the Riviera wouldn't beat it. Not when the person sitting across from you was the most beautiful and wonderful man who had ever lived.

Jessica stopped at the top of the stairs and wrapped her arms around her husband. Neither of them had really tasted their food, they'd been so busy gazing at each other and kissing over the napkin dispenser and bottle of ketchup. It didn't matter, though; the only thing Jessica was hungry for was Mike.

"I love you so much," Jessica whispered. "Please, let's never argue like that again."

Mike held her close. "Your wish is my command, baby, you know that," he whispered back. "All I want is for everyone to know you're mine, that's all. Is that too much to ask?"

"No," she murmured, her lips against his neck. "That's not too much at all."

His mouth was hot against hers. "Let's go home," Mike said. "Let's go home and forget today ever happened."

Wrapped in each other's arms, they walked down the stairs and headed for the bike. Jessica was half-lost in a dreamy haze as they walked across the parking lot, when she saw herself coming out of the ladies' room of the adjoining gas station. *That can't be me,* she told herself. *I'd never wear a dress like that.*

She pulled Mike to a stop. "Look!" she cried. "There's my sister! There's Elizabeth!"

"What's she doing way out here?" Mike asked.

Jessica shook her head. "I don't know. I don't see the Jeep . . ."

"Maybe she's stuck on the highway," Mike suggested. "We better offer her a lift."

Jessica was about to call out to her twin when she saw Elizabeth stop beside a guy filling up a silver convertible.

"It's all right," Jessica said. She nodded toward pump 3. "She must be with him."

Mike's body stiffened. "Isn't that William White?" he asked in a flat, hard voice.

Jessica looked again. There was no mistaking that blond hair and moon-shadow-pale skin. There was no mistaking the rigid way he carried himself, either. "Yes," she said. "That's William White."

Mike's hand tightened around her waist. "I thought I warned you about him," he said. "What's your sister doing hanging out with a piece of work like that?"

Jessica looked at him, surprised by the intensity of feeling in his words. "I didn't know you were so serious," she said. "I thought you just didn't like him."

Mike started walking again, pulling her toward where they'd parked. "I don't like him. I don't like him at all."

"But shouldn't we say hello to Elizabeth?" she asked.

He let go of her. "You can if you want," he said. "I'll wait for you at the bike."

Chapter Six

"So where's your mom this morning?" Elizabeth asked as she and Nina entered the cafeteria. "I got the impression she doesn't like leaving you on your own."

Nina laughed. She still had a few faint bruises from the attack, but it was clear to Elizabeth that the shock was wearing off. Nina was almost back to her old self.

"She doesn't," Nina said. She made a face. "You should see what I go through just to get away from her to visit Bryan in the hospital for a few minutes once a day. Luckily she's having breakfast with the dean of students this morning."

"Why? Is she checking up on you?" Elizabeth teased. "Does she suspect your grade-point average is only 3.9?"

Nina laughed. "She said it's because she wants to know what the university is going to do about what happened, but I think she's checking up on Bryan. The way she talks about him, you'd think he was some kind of bomb-throwing radical."

Elizabeth nodded sympathetically. Without even thinking about it, she'd begun to take the freedom of living on campus for granted. As hard as it had been for Elizabeth to adjust to university life, she was now so accustomed to making her own decisions without having to get her parents' approval that she didn't even think about it anymore. *I guess this is what being grown up is really all about,* she thought as they joined the breakfast line.

"At least your parents care," Elizabeth consoled her. "Look at Celine. I don't think she's gotten as much as a postcard since school started." She gave Nina a smile. "Then again, maybe even her family realizes what a pain in the butt she is," she added.

Nina laughed, but the laugh quickly turned into a sigh. "To tell you the truth, Elizabeth, having my mother around is kind of like living in a police state. I can't go out for half an hour without her wanting to know where I've been. I can't pick up a magazine without her wanting to know what I'm reading."

Elizabeth took a bowl of muesli from the counter and poured skimmed milk over it. "At least she's staying in a hotel off-campus," she teased. "Think how much worse it would've been if she'd gotten a room in the dorm."

"I'd have put on ten pounds by now," Nina groaned. "The other thing about having my mother around is that I get so nervous she makes me want to eat all the time."

Elizabeth passed Nina the milk. "So that's why you wanted to have breakfast with me—so I'd keep you on your diet."

"Of course," Nina said. "You didn't think it was because I missed you, did you? It was because we're committed to the same minimal caloric intake."

Elizabeth led the way to an empty table. "Well, maybe you haven't missed me," she said as they set down their trays, "but I've missed you. Now that Tom and I aren't really speaking, I have no one to discuss anything with. Having your mother around may be nerve-racking, but sharing a room with Celine is like living with a double agent. I'm afraid to leave anything in the room when I'm not there, because she's always snooping through my stuff."

Like the best friend she was, Nina went straight to the heart of the matter. "How come you and Tom aren't speaking?" she asked.

While they slowly chewed their way through the muesli, Elizabeth explained about her falling-out with Tom. "The ironic thing is that William doesn't want to hear about my investigation, either. He doesn't believe the secret society exists."

Nina started to peel an orange. "Of course it exists," she said shortly. "Everyone's heard the rumors. Even my mother's heard them, and she's only been here a couple of days." She gave Elizabeth a rueful smile. "And I've done more than hear about it. I've felt it."

Elizabeth nodded. "I know. How can William not have heard about it? He thinks Tom's making the whole thing up just to frighten me."

Nina stopped in mid-peel. "To frighten you out of doing the story?"

"I guess." Elizabeth shrugged.

Nina glanced at Elizabeth over her orange. "I told you Tom likes you. If he is making it up, he's just trying to protect you."

Elizabeth sipped her coffee. "Maybe . . ."

William's remark last night about the anonymous letter, that she only had Tom's word about it, made her feel distinctly uneasy, and it was an uneasiness that wasn't going away.

"There's something you're not telling me," Nina said. "Come on, Elizabeth. What is it?"

Elizabeth sighed and told her what William had said. "I can't decide what he was trying to suggest," she finished. "I mean, William's made it pretty clear that he's not a big Tom Watts fan. If he thinks that Tom invented this threatening letter to make me stop investigating, it wasn't to protect me. It was something else."

Nina licked orange juice from her fingers. "You mean he thinks Tom's involved?"

Elizabeth shook her head. Last night, as she tossed and turned, trying to get to sleep, she'd come to the same conclusion: that William was suggesting Tom was involved in the secret society. But she'd rejected that possibility last night, too.

"It's impossible," Elizabeth said. "It's just totally impossible. Tom's as likely to be involved with those cretins as you and I. If it's anybody we know, it's got to be Peter Wilbourne."

"Now all you have to do is prove it," Nina said.

Elizabeth picked up her coffee cup again. She'd given this some thought last night as well. Nina had recognized the voice of one of her assailants. All they had to do was match it to a name and face, and even if he wasn't the leader, they would be on their way to finding out who the leader was.

"You mean all *we* have to do is prove it," Elizabeth said.

Todd clapped Winston on the shoulder as they took their sandwiches and drinks over to a corner table in the snack bar. "You know," he said, "we should do this more often, Winston. I haven't seen enough of you since we've been at SVU."

Winston sat down, looking as though he wasn't quite sure how to respond. "I did bump into you at the pizza place last week," he said.

Todd laughed. He'd seen so little of Winston since September that he'd almost forgotten how funny and easy to be with he was. That was what he'd always liked about Winston.

"It's a shame when old friends drift apart," Todd said. He picked up his cheeseburger. "We should try not to let that happen to us."

Winston smiled nervously. "Well," he said, trying unsuccessfully to pick up his tuna-and-sprouts sandwich and keep the filling in it at the same time, "I guess you and I haven't been traveling in the same circles much."

Todd's smile tightened slightly. "No, I guess we haven't," he answered, his eyes on his lunch. With all the furor over the athletics scandal, he couldn't help wondering if Winston was being a little sarcastic. After all, until the scandal Todd had been a big man on campus, hanging out with the other superjocks, while Winston was just Winston living in an all-girls dorm.

Sprouts dropped to the table. "I guess it hasn't helped that I didn't get into the Sigmas," Winston said.

Todd looked over with relief. Winston wasn't being sarcastic, he was just telling the truth.

"Are you kidding?" Todd asked. "You think I care whether or not you're in a fraternity?"

Winston scooped up the sprouts with the air of a man who had done this a million times before and put them back between the slices of bread. "No, of course not." He shrugged. "I guess it's just that I still do a little." He grinned. "It's funny how things work out, isn't it? I really thought I was going to change my image and become a BMOC when I got here, but here I am, just the way I used to be." Something that looked like pickle fell into Winston's lap.

Tell me about it, Todd felt like saying. *You think things turned out differently for you, just look at me.* Todd had arrived on campus full of excitement and big plans. He'd thought he and Elizabeth would start having a more adult relationship in college, but he'd been wrong. He was so disappointed and frustrated, he'd broken off the relationship completely.

As a varsity athlete he'd thought he had it made, that he was the hottest thing since the invention of the microwave, but he'd wrong about that, too. Now he'd be lucky to stay on and not lose his scholarship.

"There's nothing wrong with the way you are," Todd said, trying to think of another topic of conversation. Part of the reason he'd invited Winston to lunch was that he was tired of being with the other jocks and doing nothing but talk about what might or might not happen to him. The other part was that he thought it might cheer him up to spend time with Winston because Winston was so ordinary. Todd was in some trouble now, but at least he knew he wasn't ordinary.

Winston looked up from his sandwich. "Hey," he said, pointing behind Todd, "isn't that your girlfriend?"

For just the smallest fraction of a second, Todd thought that Winston meant Elizabeth, but then he realized how ridiculous that was. Elizabeth Wakefield wasn't his girlfriend anymore; Lauren Hill was. Todd turned around. Lauren and several of her friends were walking behind them. Lauren was laughing.

Lately, she didn't laugh around him very much. She hadn't said anything, but he sensed that she was embarrassed by the scandal. Being the girlfriend of a superjock with an unending social life was one thing; being the girlfriend of a suspended basketball player who spent his free time sitting in his room worrying was something else. Lauren didn't see him, and he didn't call to her.

"Yeah, that's Lauren," Todd was saying as he turned back to Winston. "Isn't she some—" He broke off in midsentence because Winston was no longer talking to him. Standing beside average, ordinary Winston, her arm around his shoulders and her head bent to his, was one of the most beautiful girls Todd had ever seen.

Winston peered out from the curtain of the girl's dark hair that half-covered his face. "Do you know Denise?" he asked Todd. "Denise Waters. Denise, Todd Wilkins."

Todd shut his mouth. "I think I've seen you around," he said. Remembering his manners, he indicated the empty chair. "Maybe you'd like to join—"

"Can't," Denise said. She stood up straight. "I've got to go." She gave Winston a kiss on the cheek. "See you later, Winnie. Don't be late."

Todd just sat there for a moment, watching Winston try to stuff the rest of his sandwich into his mouth without further loss, as Denise Waters floated out, every man in the snack bar except for Winston and the grill chef watching her leave.

"You're right," Todd said. "It really is funny how things turn out."

"It's me, isn't it?" Isabella asked, staring forlornly into her cup. "It's something about me." She pouted. "Maybe he's discovered that I don't cut my toenails or that there's insanity in my family."

Danny laughed. "Isabella, come on. You know that's not true."

"Yes, it is." She picked up her spoon and slowly stirred her coffee. "Every Christmas when they put up the lights in town, my aunt Marsha would get dressed up in this silver ball gown and dance down Main Street. She thought she was in New Orleans and it was Mardi Gras."

"You could try that," Danny suggested.

"That might catch his attention."

"Maybe you're right," Isabella said. "He'd probably do a feature on it for WSVU." She grimaced. "Only, with my luck he'd have Elizabeth cover it."

"He's got a lot on his mind at the moment," Danny said loyally. "That's all it is."

"No, it isn't," Isabella said. "John F. Kennedy had a lot on his mind, and he still noticed Marilyn Monroe."

Danny took another mouthful of brownie. "The way Tom is, he wouldn't have noticed her, either," he assured her.

Isabella gave him a grateful smile. "Stop trying to cheer me up," she ordered.

Her usual problem with men was getting them to leave her alone, not getting them to notice she was alive. She sighed. "He thinks I'm frivolous, doesn't he? He doesn't take me seriously." She lowered her head, trying to catch her reflection in the napkin dispenser. "Maybe if I wore glasses," she mused. "Or pulled my hair back in one of those really tight buns, you know, so I looked more intellectual . . ."

Danny reached over and lifted her chin. "Listen to me, will you? There's nothing wrong with you, Izzy. You're intelligent, you're funny, you're kind and generous . . ." His brown eyes were staring so intensely into hers that she could see herself reflected in them. His voice became softer, and as warm as the feel of his hand on her face. "There isn't a man in his right mind who wouldn't be happy just to have you smile at him. If Tom doesn't appreciate you, it's his tough luck."

Isabella had the peculiar sensation of being lost in time. For a few seconds, while she and Danny looked into each other's eyes, she felt as though the coffeehouse had vanished, dissolving into nothing and leaving just the two of them alone at the round wooden table. She had the sudden urge to say to him, *What about you?* but she made the urge go away. Danny wasn't interested in her like that. He was her buddy, her pal, one of her best friends—and that's the way it would always be.

Suddenly he was looking at the antique clock on the wall and jumping to his feet. "I can't believe it," he said, putting some money on the table. "I've got four minutes to get to calc tutoring." He leaned over and kissed the top of her head. "Look, I'll catch you later, all right? Maybe we can work out a way to lure Tom out next Saturday night, when they're having the dance for Parents' Weekend. His folks won't be here, either."

"How about dinner tonight? I have some pasta salad in the fridge."

"I'll be over by seven thirty," Danny called as he hurried out of the café. "I'll bring the bread."

Isabella watched Danny dash through the

door and down the path. *I'm not interested in him*, she told herself. *I like Tom. Danny and I are just good friends.*

Jessica put the tray of ketchup-smeared dishes and half-finished drinks on the counter and picked up the order for table 2.

"The onion rings will be ready in ninety seconds," Hector, the grill chef, informed her. "Don't let them sit here getting cold."

Jessica nodded, too busy to speak, and headed back out on the floor.

But though Jessica's body was waiting on tables and her voice seemed incapable of saying anything more than "What can I get you?" her mind was actually having a long and involved conversation with the girls at table 6. The girls at table 6 were all Thetas, but it was Alison Quinn who was doing most of the talking in her imaginary conversation. Alison was begging Jessica to bring Mrs. Wakefield shopping with the Thetas. Alison was promising that after they went shopping, they'd have their nails done and go somewhere for lunch where there was good music and lots of cute guys. *I'm sorry*, Jessica was saying as she served the couple at table 2 their pecan pie and double espressos, *but it's out of the question, Alison. My mother doesn't want to waste her time with a bunch of frivolous, immature, naive, snobby sorority girls. She isn't inter-*

ested in loud music or cute guys. You have to try to understand how it is being a married woman, Alison, Jessica was saying in her head, *we have so many important things to talk about that teenage girls just wouldn't understand . . .*

Another explosion of laughter from the frivolous, immature, naive, and snobby sorority girls at table 6 filled the room.

Jessica groaned to herself as she went back for the onion rings. How part of her longed to be frivolous again. Frivolous and naive. Jessica slid the onion rings and the blue cheese brochette onto her tray.

Well, not totally naive. Now that she knew what it was like to lose herself in Mike's love, she wouldn't want to live without it. "But I could happily live without some of the other stuff," she muttered as she crossed the café. The fights. The jealousy. The having to account for every minute of her time and who she talked to and what they said. And why she hadn't told anyone they were married yet.

Jessica watched Danny leave the coffeehouse and the way Isabella's eyes followed him out. *It's so much fun when you're just dating and fooling around,* she thought. *Before everything gets so serious . . .*

"Hey, Jess, can I pay you?"

Jessica blinked. Without her noticing, Isabella had gotten up from her table and was standing in front of her, waving her bill in Jessica's face.

"What? Oh, sure." Jessica led the way to the cash register. "I didn't know you were going out with Danny," she said conversationally.

Isabella shook her head. "I'm not. He's just a friend." She smiled. "I've got my eye on someone else."

"That's nice," Jessica said, thinking about the fight that would occur if Mike caught her having coffee with another man. He wasn't that happy about her having female friends, never mind male ones.

Isabella put her change in her pocket. "So what about it?" she asked. "You want to move back in Thursday night or Friday morning? When do your parents descend? I've already un-made your bed so you'll feel right at home."

Jessica shut the drawer of the cash register. "I can't. I'll bring them over to see the dorm and everything, but I can't really move back in."

"Not for *two* days? Why not?"

"I just can't, that's all." Jessica picked up her pad and pencil.

Isabella's gray eyes took on a slightly stormy quality. "It's Mike, isn't it? He won't let you." The way she said it made it sound as though Mike was holding Jessica prisoner against her will.

"It's not that he won't let me, Isabella," Jessica answered, immediately defensive. "It's just that I can't."

Isabella pressed her lips together. "Can't? What does that mean, can't?"

Jessica stared back at her helplessly. *Tell her now,* a voice in her head was urging, the voice of Michael McAllery. *Tell her that you're married. Then she'll understand.* Jessica started to walk away. "I'm really busy, Izz—I've got to go."

But Isabella was even more stubborn than Jessica remembered. "Why won't he let you?" she demanded. "What kind of hold does this creep have on you?"

Jessica bridled. "He's not a creep," she said sharply. She tossed her hair over her shoulder. "And the only hold he has is that I love him."

Elizabeth shut her notebook with a snap. "Well, I guess that does it," she said. "Thanks a lot, Winston; you've really been a big help."

Winston shrugged and grinned at her. "I look at it this way, Elizabeth. You saved my life, so I answer your questions. It's a fair deal. Just make sure that if you do discover that Peter Wilbourne's the head of this organization, you won't tell him I helped you out."

She tapped her pen against the cover of her book. "A good reporter never reveals her sources," she assured him, getting to her feet.

"Where are you going now?" Winston gestured toward the library. "I'm meeting Denise over there in ten minutes and we're going to shoot some pool. You want to come?"

Elizabeth shook her head. "No, thanks. I've been so busy lately with school and the station I haven't seen my brother Steven in ages. I thought I might go over to see him and Billie this afternoon."

As she waved good-bye and watched Winston lope across the quad to meet Denise, Elizabeth couldn't help think that some things were turning out right after all. Winston was back to his old self and things were looking good between him and Denise. And Nina really was going to be fine.

And I'm not doing so badly either, Elizabeth thought as she walked to the bus stop. *I'm over Todd, I've lost some weight, I'm dating one of the most interesting men on campus . . .* She fumbled in her pocket for change as the bus pulled up. She didn't want to think about the man she *wasn't* dating—or the uncomfortable feeling she sometimes had about the man she was dating.

Elizabeth took a seat at the back, next to the window, her thoughts turning to her sister. Why hadn't Jessica said hello at the gas station last night? Elizabeth hadn't seen her and Mike, but William had. As soon as she reached the car he pointed them out. "You'd think she'd say hello," William had said. "Unless she's got enough sense to be embarrassed to be seen with Mike McAllery."

The vehemence of William's statement had surprised Elizabeth. She couldn't imagine that

William White's path would have ever crossed Mike McAllery's. William White was the type of man who ran poetry evenings and had a season ticket to the opera. Mike McAllery was the type who terrorized small towns by riding in on a 1000-cc motorcycle and making a play for the sheriff's daughter. "You don't have to eat the apple to know it's rotten," William had said when she pushed him about his connection with Mike. "McAllery isn't civilized. He lives by his own rules, and that makes him dangerous."

Elizabeth was still thinking about Jessica and Mike McAllery as she got off the bus and crossed the street. She was almost at the stairs leading into the building when she realized that there was someone coming out the door. Someone tall and dark, with a glint in his golden eyes.

"Elizabeth Wakefield!"

Elizabeth stopped. He was smiling at her. Michael McAllery was smiling at *her*. Smugly, arrogantly, with total contempt.

"Jessica's not home yet," he said, his smile growing bigger. "But she should be back soon."

Elizabeth couldn't answer. The words *Jessica* and *home* were tumbling through her brain so fast and so furiously that there wasn't room for anything else.

"If you want, you can wait upstairs for her." He held out his keys. "It's 2A."

"No . . . no . . . no, thank you," Elizabeth

stammered. "I didn't—I didn't come to see Jess. I—I came to see Steven, my brother."

He was still smiling, but the eyes were suddenly serious. "You didn't come to see Jessica?"

Elizabeth shook her head, forcing herself to walk past him. "No," she repeated. "I didn't. I came to see Steven."

He held the door open with his arm, positioning it just low enough to block her way.

"Excuse me," Elizabeth said, trying to get past him.

He wouldn't budge. "Why didn't you come to see Jessica?" he asked.

"So what did you say when he asked you why you hadn't come to see Jess?" Steven asked.

Elizabeth took the cup of tea Billie handed her. "I didn't say anything," she answered. "I was so surprised . . ."

Steven nodded. He put down his own cup and leaned back in his chair. "I should have told you they were living together, I guess," he admitted slowly. "But I didn't want you to worry."

The blue-green eyes flashed. "You don't think I'm going to worry now?" she asked, her voice not revealing the anger he could see in her eyes.

"Well, of course—" Steven began.

"At least if you'd told me earlier, I could've tried to talk Jessica out of it," she said, reminding him of Billie. "I could've tried. If nothing else, I could've let Jessica know that I'm here for her."

"I was here for her," Steven protested, aware that Elizabeth and Billie were exchanging a *You know men* look over the plate of cookies on the coffee table. Steven ran his hand through his hair. "I did what I thought was best, Elizabeth. I thought I could handle the situation."

"He's been driving me crazy," Billie said, sitting down beside Elizabeth. "Ever since Jess moved in with Mike, Steven's been creeping around like a detective."

Steven sank farther back into his chair. Women were like sharks: the minute they smelled blood, they all ganged up on you.

Elizabeth leaned toward him. "You have tried to talk to Jessica, right?" she asked. "You let her know she could turn to you if she needed to?"

"Of course I have," Steven said indignantly. What did she think he was, a complete bozo?

"They can't say hello without shouting at each other," Billie informed her. "Steven's tormented her so many times she wouldn't come up here if she was starving and wanted to borrow a crust of bread."

Elizabeth sighed. "Oh, Steven . . ."

"It's not my fault," he snapped back. "I didn't tell her to move in with El Creepo. You know how headstrong Jessica's always been."

"What about Mom and Dad?" Elizabeth asked.

What about them? he felt like saying. *You want to call them now so they can yell at me, too?*

"I haven't told them either, obviously, if that's what you're asking."

"I'm asking what happens when they get here on Friday. Are we going to tell them what's going on, or are we going to cover for Jess?"

Billie bit into a cookie. "That's a tricky one," she said to Elizabeth. "If we tell them now, they'll be upset that we didn't tell them before."

Elizabeth nodded. "But if we don't tell them, and they find out later, they're going to be really angry."

"That's true," Billie said. "But if we don't tell them now, there might still be time to persuade Jessica to move back with Isabella and your mom and dad will never have to know."

"Are you going to ask me what I think?" Steven asked. "Or are you two just going to take over here?"

Billie and Elizabeth gave each other the thumbs-up sign. "We're taking over," they said together.

Tom decided to get himself a cup of coffee at the snack bar. He was tired of sitting at his desk, staring at a blank computer screen while his mind went back and forth, trying to figure out what to do about Elizabeth and the secret society.

"If they sold rat poisoning, I might take some

of that, too," he muttered to himself as he left the studio. "At least that would solve one problem."

The snack bar was brightly lit and crowded. From the sound of it everyone was happy and having a wonderful time.

Don't any of these people have problems? Tom wondered as he forced himself through the door and into the noisy room. He slipped his hand into his pocket as he walked to the counter, feeling for the thin strip of white paper among his change. It was still there.

Tom ran his finger over the paper as though the message on it were written in Braille. *The wise man knows when to stop,* it said. This afternoon when he got to WSVU there was a fortune cookie sitting on top of his computer, and that was the message inside it. The wise man knows when to stop.

I don't know why they sent it to me, Tom thought. *It's pretty clear I'm not wise. I'm the biggest fool around.* And a crazy one at that. How could he protect Elizabeth and protect himself at the same time?

If he took the threats he'd received to the administration or the police, not only would his own involvement come out, but the society would be even more bent on revenge. If he did nothing, Elizabeth would continue with her investigation. Even if she didn't succeed, they would almost certainly both be hurt. If she did succeed, she would know the truth about him *and* they'd both be hurt. But if he could somehow stop her from going on with it, even if she lost all respect for him, at least she'd be safe.

The girls in front of Tom were talking about Parents' Weekend. The one with the green streaks in her hair was describing to the other girl what her mother was going to do when she saw her. They were both laughing.

Tom stared ahead of him at the rows of cakes and doughnuts, the baskets of potato and tortilla chips, the bowl of fruit.

What would his father tell him if he were here? What would his father think he should do?

Tom put a cup of coffee and a slice of pie on his tray. He was so sure of what his father would tell him to do that he could almost hear his father's voice. *What's most important to you?* his father would say.

"Elizabeth," Tom answered immediately and aloud.

Then what's your problem?

Tom sighed. He'd never listened much to his father's advice when he was alive; why should he start listening to it now?

Tom paid for his food and looked around for a table. In the corner Celine Boudreaux and Peter Wilbourne were sitting so close together they looked as if they were joined at the hip.

The first smile he'd allowed himself all day

settled onto Tom's lips. Celine Boudreaux and Peter Wilbourne. How could he have been so blind? The natural place to start investigating the secret society was with Peter. And the natural place to start investigating Peter was with Celine.

Tom headed for the farthest side of the snack bar so that he'd have to pass Celine's table. She was leaning against Peter and laughing, but her eyes were on Tom. He smiled. Celine smiled back.

Tom reached into his pocket, took out the strip of fortune, and tossed it into the nearest trash bin. *A wise man does what's right, not what's expedient.* That's what his father would have said.

All I want is a meal I don't have to serve, a hot bath, and a snuggle on the couch with my honey, Jessica told herself as she dragged her body up the stairs to 2A.

She put her ear to the door before she put her key in the lock. The apartment was silent; that meant Mike wasn't home yet. The first thing Mike did when he got in was put on music. She could always tell what sort of mood he was in by the CD that was playing. If it was reggae, he was in a party mood. If it was rock 'n' roll, he was feeling good and probably wanted to take out the bike or the Corvette to test radar traps. If it was the blues, he'd had a bad day. If it was classical, he just wanted to be with her.

Jessica turned the key and pushed open the door. Mike was sitting on the sofa, staring at the opposite wall.

"I didn't think you were here!" she cried, dropping her things and running over to him. "You don't have any music on."

He glanced over, his eyes as hard as gold. "How observant. Maybe you should think about going to college, a smart girl like you."

"What's the matter?" Jessica asked, putting her arms around him. "Did you have a bad day on the Buick?"

"No, I had a good day on the Buick." He shook her off. "I didn't start having a bad day till I came back here."

She sat back, looking at him even though he was pointedly not looking at her. She could tell from the set of his jaw and the tenseness of his body that it was more than just a bad day. He was ready to explode.

"Well, I've had a terrible day," she said. She started to get up. "I'm going to soak in the tub for a while."

"No, you're not." He reached out and pulled her back down so quickly that she screamed. "You're staying right here."

"Mike!" She wrenched her arm free. "What's wrong with you? You're not drunk, are you?"

He turned to face her. "No," he said, slowly and carefully pronouncing each word. "I am not drunk. I am painfully sober, as it happens. I've never been so sober in my life."

She touched his shoulder. "Then what's wrong? Why are you so angry?"

"Me?" He lifted her hand from him. "Why am I so angry?"

Jessica nodded, but her heart was beginning to beat hard. For the first time since she'd known Mike, she was really afraid that he might hit her.

"I'll tell you, Jessica," he said, his voice as calm and even as an anchorman's while reading the news. "I'll tell you exactly why I'm so angry. I saw your sister today."

"Elizabeth?" Where would Mike have run into Elizabeth? What had he said to her? Jessica's blood went cold. What if he told her they were married? She forced herself to choke out the next question. "Where?"

"Downstairs." He smiled. "She was visiting your brother."

"Oh, right, she was visiting Steven." Jessica smiled, too, but her smile, unlike Mike's, wasn't loaded with venom. It was loaded with relief. At least Elizabeth hadn't been looking for *her*.

He tilted his head to one side, studying her face. "How come she wasn't visiting you, Jess?" he asked. "How come she wasn't visiting *us*?"

Jessica's mouth opened, but there was nothing she could say. He knew why Elizabeth wasn't visiting them. She didn't know there was anyone to visit. She didn't know Jessica was living with Mike, let alone that they were married.

"You haven't told anybody, have you?" His voice started rising. "Not one single person." He stood up, kicking the leather hassock out of his way. "I've told everybody I know, Jess. My clients, the guys I play pool with, the guys at the bar. I even told the girl in the deli where I buy my lunch—*hey, guess what I did yesterday, I got married*—but you haven't told anybody."

"I'm going to Mike, I—"

This time he kicked the coffee table. A half-empty glass crashed to the floor and several magazines flew across the room.

"Why not?" He was shouting in earnest now, madder than Jessica had ever seen him. "Why haven't you told anyone? What's going to happen when your parents get here Friday? Are you planning to introduce me as your roommate, Isabella Ricci? Don't you think I'm a little tall?"

"They're not coming," Jessica blurted out, which was almost true. They weren't coming Friday as they'd planned but on Saturday. Mrs. Wakefield had an unexpected but important meeting to attend for work. "Isabella told me today. They called last night and they can't make it," she went on in a rush, amazed that her brain could still work when her heart was falling apart. "My father's got to go to New York on business."

Mike picked up a coffee mug and threw it

across the room. "I don't care!" he raged. "That's not the point. The point is that you haven't told them I'm your husband! Why not?" There were tears in his eyes. "Why, Jess? Why?"

There were tears in her eyes, too. "Because I'm afraid they'll try to break us up," she sobbed, sounding so sincere that she almost convinced herself she was telling the truth. "You don't know my father. He's a powerful lawyer, Mike. He—"

"I don't care if he's the president. You're my wife. That's all that matters. Nobody can change that but you and me."

Jessica threw herself into Mike's arms. "I love you so much," she whispered, her words thick and choked. "Please don't leave me. I love you."

He put his head on her shoulder. "I love you, too, baby," he whispered. His tears were hot and salty on her neck.

Chapter
Seven

Nina stopped in the doorway to Bryan's hospital room. Bryan was not only sitting up in bed, he was working on a laptop computer and singing along to the song playing on the radio.

"Well, you're looking a lot better," she said, stepping into the room.

At the sound of her voice Bryan looked up, grinning. "And you always look good."

Nina held up the bag she was carrying. "I couldn't stand the thought of you wasting away in here with nothing to eat but hospital food, so I brought you breakfast."

Bryan sniffed the air. "Doughnuts, if my nostrils aren't deceiving me. Fresh doughnuts." He sniffed again. "Chocolate, jelly, and cinnamon."

She put the bag on the bed beside him and sat down in the visitor's chair. "How did you know that?"

"They may have broken my bones, but the nose is intact." He opened the bag and looked inside. "The real question is, How did you know these are my favorites?"

"I guess you must have mentioned it," Nina answered, leaning over to fix the lace on her shoe so he couldn't see her blushing.

"It was nice of you to remember." He held the doughnuts out to her. "So where does your mother think you are?"

Nina looked into the bag. She didn't normally eat doughnuts, since they weren't on her diet, but she didn't normally lie to her mother, either.

"She thinks I had an eight o'clock class," Nina answered, helping herself.

"She's not going to be too happy if she finds out you've been sneaking over here to see me," Bryan said.

"At least my mother doesn't think you're an enemy of the state anymore." Nina licked some sugary glaze from her fingers. "The dean of students gave you such a big buildup that she actually said she'd like to meet you."

Bryan pretended to choke on his doughnut. "You're kidding! Your mother wants to meet *me?*"

As bizarre as it seemed, it was true. Grace Harper had come back from her breakfast with Dean Lombardi full of all the good things she'd learned about Bryan. Did Nina know Bryan was a straight-A student? Did Nina know that Bryan had been president of his senior class in high school? Did she know that Bryan had won three different scholarships and several prestigious achievement awards? Did Nina know that Bryan had received a special commendation from the governor for volunteer work he'd done with children in the inner city?

Nina nodded. "My mother said you sound, and I quote, 'like a very special young man.'"

"If you don't disillusion her, does that mean she won't make you go back with her?"

"We've been talking about it a lot. She and my dad still want me to leave . . ." Nina crumbled the piece of doughnut she was still holding, watching the bits spill across her lap.

"But?"

Nina looked up to find that Bryan had moved to the edge of the bed, his hazel eyes studying her closely.

"But I've realized that it's my life and it's my decision. I have a scholarship; if I want to stay, they really can't stop me." Nina searched for the right words to express all that she'd been thinking. "As much as I love them, I'm not like my parents. They wanted to be successful and comfortable, but I want something more." She smiled into those eyes. "I guess I want to fight for what I believe in."

Bryan leaned forward, his face only inches from hers. "When you say *stay*, do you mean until the end of the semester or do you mean for good?"

"I guess I mean for good," Nina said.

"That's what I was hoping you meant," Bryan whispered as his lips found hers.

Jessica sat in the front seat of the Buick that Mike was working on, a lilac notepad on her lap. After they made up last night, she'd lain awake for hours, trying to decide what to do next.

She had to keep Mike away from her parents until she'd had a chance to talk to them herself. But at the same time, she had to keep Mike happy and believing that her parents knew about him.

And then she'd come up with a brilliant idea. She'd write them a letter. She and Mike would compose it together, and he'd be satisfied that she was doing what she'd promised. He'd watch her write it, sign it, and seal it—but he wouldn't watch her mail it. Because it was going straight into the garbage can at the coffeehouse as soon as she got to work. Then she could sneak off to see her parents on Saturday while Mike was working, and decide what to do from there.

"This is what I've got so far," she called to

Mike. *"Dear Mom and Dad, I know it's been a while since I wrote to you, but a lot has been happening in my life since I've been at college. I guess this is going to come as a surprise, but I've fallen in love!"*

Mike came over with a toolbox in his hands and leaned against the door. "Sounds good so far."

He tried to peer over her shoulder, but she playfully pushed him away. "Get away from me; you're all greasy. I still have to go to work today."

Laughing, he pointed to the letter. "What's all that stuff that you didn't read?"

"That's all the boring stuff about how wonderful and sensitive and talented and heartbreakingly gorgeous you are," she said airily. "You wouldn't be interested in it."

"Yes, I would." He grabbed the pad from her at the same time that he handed her the toolbox.

"Mike!" Jessica squealed. "Now I'm all filthy."

Mike didn't hear her. He was reading the letter with a big smile on his face. "You do say I'm wonderful," he said, sounding as excited as a little kid on Christmas morning.

"Of course I do." She reached up to pull him toward her and kissed a clean spot on his cheek. "You're the most wonderful mechanic in the whole world."

He made an unhappy face. "You haven't told them that we're married, though."

Jessica took a deep breath. Simple, straightforward schemes usually worked better than the more complicated variety, but this time she couldn't keep it simple. "You said you wanted to drive out to Sweet Valley and meet them, remember? I thought it would be better if we told them in person."

"You're right, Mrs. McAllery." He kissed her as he handed her back the letter. "You're absolutely right. I want to see their faces when they find out."

"Me too," Jessica said, forcing herself to match Mike's smile. "I can hardly wait."

Elizabeth let out a shriek of joy as she and Nina left the English building together. "I can't believe it," she said, turning to her friend with a gigantic smile. "You're really going to stay?"

Nina nodded, blushing at the thought of the morning she'd spent with Brian. She hadn't been expecting Bryan to kiss her—she certainly hadn't expected him to kiss her like that, with more passion and tenderness than she'd ever imagined—but when he had, she'd known that she'd made the right decision. Her adult life started here, at SVU, not in some Ivy League school on the East Coast, or some sleepy little campus somewhere else in California.

"Now all I have to do is tell my mother," Nina said. She smiled wryly. "At least I don't have to tell my dad, though. My mother will do that for me about three minutes after I've told her."

Elizabeth slipped her arm through Nina's. "I'll tell you what—why don't we share a piece of the triple-chocolate cake they have at the coffeehouse to celebrate? My treat."

Nina was watching four boys enter the snack bar across the quad from where they stood, a thoughtful frown on her face. "I've got a better idea," she said, giving Elizabeth a tug away from the direction of the coffeehouse. "Why don't we go have a diet soda in the snack bar instead?"

Elizabeth gave her a puzzled look. "Because people who are celebrating don't count calories, and because neither of us likes diet soda."

"But we both want to see if I recognize a certain person's voice from the night of the attack, don't we?" she asked, dragging Elizabeth across the lawn.

"Where is he?" she asked, looking around.

"Peter Wilbourne and some of his Sigma buddies just went into the snack bar," Nina explained. "Maybe we can pass their table or something."

"With the big mouth that jerk has, you won't have to get that close," Elizabeth said. "You'll be able to hear him from across the room."

The two girls stopped in the entrance, searching for the blue Sigma jackets among the crowd.

"I can't hear him," Nina said after a few seconds. "But I see him." Suddenly she was feeling as frightened as she was excited. "The Sigmas are over there, on the line for the grill. Let's go."

Elizabeth held her back. "Wait a minute," she said in a low voice. "I know you said you wanted to stay at SVU and fight for what you believe is right, but I'm not so sure that we want Peter Wilbourne to know that's what you're doing just yet. If I'm right about him and he knows you know he was involved in the attack, they might try to hurt you and Bryan again."

Nina nodded. "Okay. Why don't you get in line while I get straws and napkins? I should be able to hear them from over there without them seeing me."

"You're a genius," Elizabeth said. "Two diet sodas coming right up!"

Nina stood in front of the array of napkins, straws, silverware, and condiments as though trying to make up her mind. A few feet in front of her, the Sigmas discussed their preferences among pro-football teams and sorority girls. Elizabeth had been right about Peter Wilbourne's voice. It was loud and clear, easily soaring over the sounds of talk and clattering dishes. Smiling to herself, Nina took two straws and two napkins from their holders and went to find a table at the other end of the room.

*　　　*　　　*

"So Danny's going to talk Tom into going to the movies on Saturday night," Isabella was saying, "and then I'm going to bump into them at the snack counter and Danny's going to ask me to sit with them. Isn't that a great idea?"

"Brilliant," Jessica said.

"If this doesn't work, I may have to give up, though," Isabella continued. "I mean, I've given Tom several of my best shots, and so far the nicest response I've ever gotten from him is politeness." She wiped a drop of soda from the tabletop. "Maybe it's true that he really isn't interested in women," she said to the Formica. "Some men aren't."

Grateful as she was for Isabella's companionship and a chance to sit down at a table instead of waiting on it, Jessica stifled a yawn. Isabella had been talking about Danny Wyatt and Tom Watts for the last half hour. When Isabella invited her to the snack bar for a soda, Jessica thought they were going to gossip like they used to, not just talk about Isabella.

"But enough about me," Isabella said, as though reading her thoughts. "What about you, Jess? How's life in paradise? Are you still madly, head-over-heels in love, or are you beginning to realize that Mike's human after all?"

Jessica shrugged. She didn't really want to talk about herself, either. What she wanted to talk about was who was dating whom, and where, and what they were wearing while they were doing it. Those were the things that used to make her happy. "It's all right. I go to school, I go to work, I go home. You know, the usual sort of thing."

Isabella twirled her straw in her soda. "And what about Mike?" she asked, watching the ice swirl around. "How's he? Is he looking forward to meeting your parents?"

Jessica could only hope that her face hadn't gone as red as it felt. "Mike has to work on Saturday," she said, trying to sound matter-of-fact.

Isabella had a way of looking at a person that made you feel as if she were peering through a microscope. She was looking at Jessica that way now. "All day?"

"He has a big job," Jessica said. "He can't afford to take off."

"Not even at night?" Isabella asked. "You mean you two aren't going to the dance with your parents? I really wanted to see Mike dancing with your mother."

Just the thought of Mrs. Wakefield in one of her conservative dresses doing the twist with Mike made Jessica's stomach turn. "Mike's not really a dancing man," she answered. "We thought we'd let Elizabeth and that ghoul she's dating go to the dance with my parents."

Isabella smiled, but her eye was still to the microscope. "You mean you're not going to the dance because Mike hates William White," she said flatly. "That's the real reason, isn't it?"

Jessica looked back in surprise. She was surprised that there was such a convenient and truthful excuse available, but she was also surprised that Isabella knew about Mike's dislike of her sister's new boyfriend. "How did you know that?"

Isabella shook her head. "I'm not sure, really." She sipped her soda, her pretty face frowning in concentration. "I think maybe Peter Wilbourne said something about it. You know what a gossip he is." She groaned. "This is so annoying. I can't remember if he said they'd had a big fight or what, but it sounded pretty serious."

"Well, Mike definitely doesn't like him," Jessica said. "That much I'm sure of."

"It kinda scares me," Isabella said, pretending to shudder. "I don't know if I can get used to the idea of me and Mike McAllery agreeing on something, even if it is how creepy William White is."

Jessica glared at her. "I keep telling you, Izzy. You'd like Mike if you gave him a chance."

"It doesn't look like I'm going to have a chance if he's not coming with you on Saturday. Can't he even get away in the afternoon? I was going to get some cake and stuff so that we could have a snack with your parents in our room."

Jessica had been trying to think of some way to change the subject when a change of subject walked through the door. "Isabella," Jessica said, giving her a little kick under the table. "Are you sure Tom Watts isn't interested in women?"

Isabella turned in the direction Jessica was looking. At the entrance to the snack bar were Tom and Celine, standing about as close together as two people could.

"That doesn't mean he's interested in women," Isabella said. "It means he's interested in witches."

Celine smiled to herself as she strolled back to Dickenson Hall. *This has been quite a day so far,* she thought as she swished along. *Quite a day.*

Even though Tom Watts was too earnest and principled to be her type, Celine had made a play for him at the beginning of the semester. She'd done it partly because she'd known it would annoy Elizabeth, and as far as Celine was concerned anything that annoyed Elizabeth was worth doing. More than that, though, Celine considered Tom a challenge. He was as remote and aloof as he was handsome and intelligent, but even more than that he was so *good*. How wonderful it would feel to win the heart of someone as decent and respected as Tom.

162

Celine began to hum as she walked, her honey-blond hair shimmering behind her like sunlight. Despite her best efforts and considerable charms, Tom hadn't responded. Unless running in the opposite direction every time he saw her coming could be considered a response.

He hadn't responded until now.

Another smile lit up Celine's beautiful face. Now Tom Watts was pursuing her. First there was that look he'd given her when she was with Peter in the snack bar, and then there was today. Probably he'd been following her ever since, because he'd been standing right outside her dorm, not very inconspicuously, when she came out this afternoon. She'd nearly walked right past him. "What are you doing tonight?" he'd said, and before she could answer, he'd taken her arm.

Celine came to a stop at the curb, her thoughts still on Tom. He was taking her out tonight. Tom Watts never took anyone out, but tonight he was going out with her. Should she dress up or dress down? Was the Elizabeth Wakefield I-don't-flirt-I'm-an-intellectual look to be copied, or should she find the sexiest outfit she had and wear that?

She was just about to cross the street when she felt a strong male hand on her shoulder. Celine turned. Peter Wilbourne was standing beside her, catching his breath.

"Why, Peter," Celine said, her eyelids fluttering in surprise. "I didn't hear you behind me."

"What's going on, Celine? I thought you were going out with me. What were you doing in the snack bar just now with Tom?"

Her smile was as innocent as a baby's as she shifted out of his grasp and started across the road, Peter loping beside her. "I was having a cup of coffee, Peter, what did it look like I was doing?"

"It looked like you were trying to sit on his lap," he snapped. "I thought you hated that creep as much as I do, Celine. What's the deal?"

I do love jealousy, Celine was thinking while Peter ranted. *Jealousy is to love what jalapeño peppers are to chili.*

"Celine!" He yanked her to a stop. "I asked you a question. What's going on?"

Her arm wrapped itself through his and she pressed against him. "Don't be mad at me, Peter," she said, her pale-blue eyes troubled and hurt. "I thought you wanted to know what Tom and Elizabeth are up to, that's all. I thought if I sweet-talked him a little, he might tell me all."

Peter blinked. She could see this new thought lumbering through his tiny brain.

"You did?" he said. "You were doing it for me?"

She slowly brushed a strand of hair from his forehead. "Of course I was. Don't you think it's a good idea?"

"Of course it's a good idea." He smiled. "In

fact, it's a fantastic idea." He pulled her closer. "It's such a fantastic idea that I may just have to take you out for a special dinner to reward you."

"I'm afraid you'll have to reward me tomorrow," Celine whispered. "I have an exam to study for tonight."

"I meant tomorrow," Peter whispered back. "Champagne and lobster right on the ocean. How does that sound?"

"Perfect."

Celine was still saying the word *perfect* over and over to herself as she floated into Dickenson Hall and down the corridor to her room. Everything was perfect. In fact, everything was working out so well that she almost couldn't believe she hadn't planned it this way.

She'd already shut the door behind her before she saw the long, lean figure, all in black, lying like a shadow on her silk bedspread.

"You planning on sleeping with the enemy, Celine?" William asked, his smile as cold as his eyes. "Or do you have some really good reason why you've suddenly decided to snuggle up to Tom Watts?"

Celine threw her things on Elizabeth's chair. It was like her granny always said: Men are like taxis. When you need one, you can't find one; and when you don't want one, they all turn up. She took a cigarette from the pack on her desk and lit it slowly.

"I have a really good reason," Celine answered.

Elizabeth was surprised to get back to her dorm room and find Celine gone and William sitting at her desk, reading a book of Japanese poems.

"Am I late?" she asked, glancing at the clock. "I'm really sorry, William. I must have gotten the time wrong. I thought we weren't going out until later."

No matter how strange she sometimes felt about William, Elizabeth had to admit that he had an incredible smile.

"We weren't," he said, shutting the book. "But I dropped by to tell you that I can't make it after all. Celine said I could wait."

Elizabeth put down her books. "You can't make it?" She couldn't hide her disappointment. The strain of the week, especially her discovery about Jessica, was beginning to take its toll on her. She'd been looking forward to forgetting about her worries for a few hours, just listening to William talk.

"Don't look so sad, Elizabeth." William stood up and put his arms around her. "We'll go out tomorrow night if you're free. It's just that one of my professors asked me to help him with something and I couldn't say no." He looked into her face. "You understand, don't you?"

"Of course I do," Elizabeth said quickly. "It's just that I've been thinking so much about

Jessica today that I really wanted to get my mind on something else."

"What has Jessica done now?" William asked. He'd heard enough stories about Jessica to know it had to be big if Elizabeth was worried.

Elizabeth hadn't intended to tell him, but somehow the words came tumbling out with a will of their own. "She's living with Mike McAllery."

William looked at her blankly for a second, as though she'd spoken too quickly in a language he didn't know very well. "What?"

"She's living with Mike McAllery," Elizabeth repeated. "My brother told me. She's been living with him for weeks."

"What about your parents?" William was so concerned, it was as though it was his own sister they were talking about. "Do your parents know?"

Elizabeth shook her head. "Steven didn't tell them either. He seemed to think he could handle the situation himself."

"Then you have to tell them." He gestured at the telephone. "They're her parents; they have to know what's going on."

Elizabeth paused, surprised by his decisiveness. "I haven't talked to Jessica yet," she protested. "I don't want to deceive my parents, but I do think I should hear what my sister has to say first."

He seemed to consider this for a few seconds, but then he started shaking his head. "I don't think that's such a good idea, Elizabeth. From what I've heard about your sister, she can talk her way out of anything. I think you should tell your parents right away."

She didn't want to argue with him. Suddenly, all she wanted was for him to go away. With Celine out she had the room to herself; maybe she could just listen to some music and read a book and forget about everybody for a few hours.

"They'll be here Saturday," Elizabeth said, putting him off. "It can wait till then."

Instead of arguing, William nodded in agreement.

"You're right," he said. "We can tell them together if you want. At the sixties dance."

"At the dance?" Elizabeth said, too surprised to try not to show it.

He looked surprised, too. "Aren't your parents staying for the dance? Don't you want to go?"

"You haven't asked me," she reminded him.

His handsome face looked pained. "I'm sorry, Elizabeth, I don't know what got into me. I just assumed that we'd go together. We have talked about the dance . . . I thought it was understood." He took her hand in his. "I was really looking forward to spending some time with you and meeting your parents."

Elizabeth looked away, feeling slightly guilty.

Maybe she hadn't realized William was planning to take her to the dance because she was hoping someone else might ask her. "Of course I want to go with you," she said finally. "But I'll have to see how my parents feel about it."

He gave her one of his high-wattage smiles. "That's my girl."

William's girl, Elizabeth thought, wondering why the words didn't make her feel happier.

Danny held the door open for Isabella as they stepped into the night.

"I still don't think it means anything," he said as he fell into step beside her. "So Tom and Celine had a cup of coffee together, so what? Grant and Lee had a cup of coffee together once, too, and that didn't make them friends."

Isabella automatically slipped her arm through Danny's as they walked. Danny had taken her out to get her mind off seeing Tom and Celine together in the snack bar that afternoon, and he'd done such a good job of cheering her up that she hadn't given them a thought all night. Until now.

"Lee didn't look or smell like Celine Boudreaux," she said sourly. "And I bet he didn't sit as close to Grant as Tom was sitting to Celine, either."

Danny gave her a shake. "Don't get all glum on me again," he ordered. "Tom's like my brother. I'm telling you, Izzy, no matter what you saw, there's no way he's interested in Celine. She's less his type than an iguana." He grinned. "Besides, a woman who's just consumed half her weight in pineapple pizza has no right to be glum." He pointed above them. "Look at the stars! Look at the moon!"

Isabella sighed loudly. "Don't tell me," she moaned. "The night's still young."

"It is," Danny said. "We could go dancing, or take a drive out to the beach, or—"

"Play backgammon?" Isabella asked. "If I remember correctly, I backgammoned you twice last time and you were screaming for mercy."

"You're remembering it wrong," Danny answered with a laugh. "It was once, and you cheated."

"Liar!" she shouted. "You're the one who cheats all the time. Don't think I don't see you sneaking in those extra moves."

Danny stopped suddenly, slapping his forehead. "I just realized," he said, his voice now serious. "We can't possibly play backgammon."

Isabella looked at him. "Why not? You have a test to study for or something?"

He shook his head. "No ice cream, Izzy. This could be a long one. How can we play without ice cream?"

She didn't answer him. She didn't have to. They both spun around and started walking in the opposite direction, to where the ice-cream store was.

"Rum raisin or banana crunch?" Isabella asked.

"Banana crunch" came Danny's immediate reply. "I play much better on banana crunch."

"Don't get overconfident." She punched him in the chest. "You'll have to eat about three gallons if you hope to beat me."

They were still laughing fifteen minutes later as they took the shortcut across the campus to Isabella's dorm, Danny carrying the ice cream and Isabella carrying the cookies they'd decided they needed to go with it.

"No, you're wrong, Izzy," Danny was saying as they turned into the overgrown area that lay between the administration buildings and the newer dorms. "Groucho was funny—I'm not saying Groucho wasn't funny, but Chico was the star. Sometimes I just have to think of him saying, 'There ain't no Sanity Clause,' and I crack up."

"*You're* wrong," Isabella argued. "Chico was wonderful in his way, and I liked his little hat, but Groucho was the genius behind the Marx brothers. Everybody knows that."

"Not everybody," Danny said. "And don't underestimate Harpo, Izzy. Let's not forget about him."

But Isabella's mind wasn't on Harpo. Somewhere in front of them, along the dark,

171

seemingly deserted path, twigs were breaking and leaves were rustling. While Danny extolled the virtues of Harpo Marx, Isabella strained to listen to the night. Footsteps. She was sure she heard footsteps.

"Danny," she hissed, pulling him up short. "Did you hear that?"

Hearing the urgency in her voice, he froze, his hand tightening its grip on hers. The road and its lights were yards away. Immediately tense and alert, Danny tried to see into the dark. "It was probably just a bird or something," he reassured her.

Isabella wasn't so sure. "If that was a bird, it was wearing shoes," she whispered back.

There was a scuffling farther ahead of them and a low muffled sound nearby.

"The bird's moaning now," Isabella said. She started to move forward, but Danny held her back.

"Stay here. I'll go look."

Isabella took hold of his arm. "Oh, no, you don't. You're not leaving me here by myself. We'll go together."

"Be reasonable, Izzy. If someone is there, you might have to run for help."

"Run?" It wasn't the time or the place, but she really felt like laughing. "Danny, I'm wearing two-inch heels and the ground's soft. I'm not running anywhere." She held him more tightly. "I'm going with you."

This time there was no mistaking the sound: it was a person groaning.

Isabella took something out of her bag. "Here," she said, thrusting it into his hand as they cautiously tiptoed forward.

"What is it?"

"A flashlight." She stopped again. "Over there," she said, and pointed toward a clump of blackness. "I'm sure it's coming from those bushes."

"If someone jumps out at us, you kick off those heels of yours and run, you hear me?"

She gave him a shove forward. "Yes, I hear you."

Isabella held her breath as Danny turned on the tiny flashlight, shining it under the shrubs.

Isabella's eyes followed the frail beam. Rocks, twigs, a few snack wrappers, a brown work boot. "Danny!" she hissed.

But Danny was already on his knees, pushing the bushes aside. When he finally spoke, he wasn't whispering anymore, he was shouting.

Isabella's eyes fell on the face of the man lying on the ground. "Oh, my God! Tom!"

Chapter Eight

Todd came out of the breakfast line and looked around for someone to sit with. Lauren was with a group of her friends on one side of the cafeteria. There were a few of the jocks over on the other side, huddled among themselves, but Todd was tired of having breakfast with them. As the investigation dragged on, their efforts to cheer each other up and act like nothing was wrong were more and more depressing. Mark never came to meals at all anymore; he either ate in his room or went off-campus.

Todd was thinking he should probably eat in his room, too, when he spotted Enid sitting by herself at a corner table. She was crumbling a piece of toast while she read a novel. At last, a friendly face.

"Mind if I join you?" he asked, not waiting for her reply before he sat down. "Keep on reading if you want, Alex. Don't mind me. I just didn't feel like sitting alone."

Enid tossed the book aside with a sigh. "I wasn't really reading it," she admitted. "I was just looking at the words. They were making about as much sense as the Russian alphabet, if you want to know the truth."

Todd started taking his food from the tray. "You and Mark have a fight?"

Even to Todd's ears, Enid's laugh sounded a little on the hollow side.

"You mean *another* fight, don't you?" she asked. She pushed her plate away. "When I think of how happy we were at first . . ." Her voice trailed off, and she stared at her coffee cup as though watching something in the distance move farther away.

Todd turned his attention to buttering his toast.

Enid took a deep breath. "So," she said, "what about you and Lauren? Are you two okay?"

"We're okay," he said, knowing he didn't sound very convincing. He made a vague gesture toward the table where Lauren Hill's clear, cool laughter could be heard rising above the noise of the room. "Lauren's been pretty busy lately, what with midterms coming and everything."

"Oh, I know," she answered quickly. "It's a hectic time of year, especially with Parents' Weekend."

Todd didn't want to think about Parents' Weekend. Parents' Weekend should have been his finest hour. He'd pictured himself striding around campus with his parents, introducing them to all his friends, basking in their praise when they realized how popular he was and how well he was doing. Now he had nothing to show them but a blank space where his great life used to be.

"I'm not looking forward to it either," Enid said. "I was having such a good time with Mark that I let my grades slip, which isn't exactly going to thrill my mother to pieces. My mother's old-fashioned. She thinks you go to college to get educated."

It was Todd's laugh that was hollow this time. What was Alexandra worried about? At least she hadn't been suspended from the basketball team and accused of accepting bribes.

"And my mother's going to wonder why I'm not speaking to Elizabeth," Enid said. "She'll have about a million questions about that. You know what a big Elizabeth Wakefield fan my mom's always been."

"Elizabeth." Todd repeated the name as though he'd never heard it before. With all his other worries, he hadn't given any thought to the fact that his parents were going to notice that Elizabeth wasn't his girlfriend anymore.

"The way things were at the beginning of the semester, I thought that by the time my mom visited I'd be so different and doing so well, and Elizabeth would be so dowdy and dull, that she'd understand I'd outgrown Elizabeth."

"Well, it's true," Todd said. "We did outgrow her. You and I were ready to be adults, and Elizabeth wasn't. She wanted things to stay the way they were in high school."

"It doesn't look like that now," Enid said. She nodded toward the entrance to the cafeteria, where Elizabeth was talking to Danny Wyatt.

Todd looked over. Elizabeth had lost most of the weight she'd put on the first weeks of college, but more than that, she'd changed her style. There was something genuinely mature and sophisticated about her now; not in the way she dressed, but the way she was. She was stronger and more sure of herself—and determined. She looked like a young woman who was going places. He had to admit it. She looked beautiful.

"Now it looks like she's outgrown us," Enid said.

Tom opened his eyes. There was too much sunlight for it to be seven in the morning, the time he usually got up. He turned his head to the alarm clock on the table by his bed, and almost immediately his temple began to throb. Tom ignored it. He had too much to do to worry about a little headache.

"Nine o'clock!"

He couldn't believe it. What was wrong with Danny, turning off his alarm and going out and

178

letting Tom sleep till nine o'clock?

"Wait'll I get my hands on him," he muttered, jumping out of bed. Tom steadied himself against his bureau. It was difficult to ignore the pain in his leg. He'd had a bad football injury in that leg in high school, and the fall he'd taken last night must have hit him on the same spot.

Very slowly, Tom got dressed. Once he was dressed, he'd take some painkillers, and then he'd go to the studio. He and Elizabeth had put some files on the computer when they were first researching the fraternity story that might come in handy now.

"At least it's more or less out in the open," he said to his reflection in the mirror as he carefully combed his hair. "At least I know they're worried."

His reflection didn't smile back. His reflection had a cut over its eye and a bruise on the side of its forehead. It looked pretty worried, too.

He had to get Elizabeth out of the way, and he had to do it fast. It was one thing if these clowns wanted to rough him up, but he wasn't going to let them touch her.

"If they lay so much as one finger on her," Tom said to the bruised and tired-looking young man staring back at him from the glass, "if they do, I'll get every last one of them or die in the attempt."

There was a knock at the door.

"Come on in," he called, assuming it was one of

the guys on his floor, wanting to see how he was.

In the short time he'd known her, Tom had already seen several sides of Elizabeth Wakefield. He'd seen her worked up over a story. He'd certainly seen her angry, nine times out of ten with him. He'd seen her happy, too. But he'd never seen her beside herself with worry before.

She flew into the room like a small storm. "Who did this?" she demanded. "What happened? Danny was so vague . . ."

"Hello, Elizabeth," he said evenly. "And how are you on this beautiful morning?"

She threw her books on his bed and ran over to him. She put out her hand, gently touching his face.

Tom couldn't help thinking that it might not be so bad to die now, with Elizabeth Wakefield's hand on his cheek and that look of concern in her sea-green eyes.

"Look at you," she cried, but so softly that even standing inches from her he could hardly hear her. "Look what they've done to you."

He pushed her hand away. "I'm all right, Elizabeth—stop it, will you? There were only two of them, and they weren't really trying to hurt me; they just wanted me to get the message."

Elizabeth looked at his bruises for another few seconds and then, convinced that he was telling the truth, let the reporter in her start to take over. "Did you recognize them?" she wanted to know. "Do you remember anything about them that might help us identify them? What did they say?"

In spite of himself, Tom had to laugh. "Hold on, Inspector Wakefield. I thought you were worried about *me*."

She smiled, her cheeks turning pink. "I am worried about you," she said. "And I'm angry. Why didn't someone tell me last night? Why didn't you call me? Or get Danny to call me?"

All of Tom's pain disappeared in a wave of pure joy. He was a genius. He generally kept it well hidden, but he was definitely a genius. Tom smiled inwardly. All at once he knew how to keep Elizabeth away from him and the station and the secret society until he had done what he had to do.

Celine. Celine had been useful to him last night; maybe now she could be useful to him again.

"Didn't Celine tell you?" he asked innocently.

All the color drained from her face. "Celine?" Elizabeth said. "You asked Celine to tell me you'd been hurt?"

"Not exactly. It was just that it happened after I took her home last night." Which was true enough. He'd just left Celine at Dickenson Hall and was on his way to his own dorm when he was jumped from behind.

Elizabeth seemed to be having trouble understanding him. "After you took her home? Home from where?"

He had to force himself to say the words. "From our date." Elizabeth was no longer looking at him with concern. She was looking at him as though he were something legless and slimy that had appeared in her salad.

He rushed on. "I promised her I'd call her when I got back here." This was not true. This was a lie.

"You must have had a good time," Elizabeth said in a small, tight voice.

"We did," said Tom enthusiastically. This was another lie. He'd rather spend three hours in the dentist's chair than ten minutes with Celine. "But you haven't heard my great idea," Tom said, feeling inspired. "I'm going to ask Celine to work with me on the secret society piece."

"Celine?" Her voice was so small and tight now that he could barely hear her.

He shook his head. "Think about it, Elizabeth. She's got the connections."

The color began to return to her face. "But we don't need her connections," Elizabeth protested. "Nina recognized the voice. It was Peter Wilbourne. That proves it, Tom."

"That proves nothing except that he's involved, which we knew already."

"But he's obvious—"

"Exactly," Tom cut in. "He's too obvious. Whoever's running this thing is the last person you'd ever suspect. It's someone who has no ties to the Sigmas, and maybe no real ties to the college at all. It's someone smart, Elizabeth. Not a brick-brain like Peter Wilbourne. Someone really smart. A manipulator. Someone who works alone and doesn't need a bunch of goons backing him up like Peter does."

Her voice was as frosty as December in Maine. "So where does Celine and her connections come in, then?"

Tom snapped his fingers. "Celine's close enough to Peter Wilbourne to be able to take his wallet off him without him knowing," he said. "If he knows anything at all about the identity of the society's leader, she can find out. And find out without anyone suspecting a thing."

"But where do I fit in?" Elizabeth asked.

"Once we've found out what we want, you can work with Celine on writing the story, but at the moment you don't fit in anywhere." He touched his head, wincing in a little more pain than he was actually feeling. "I don't want to get roughed up again if I can help it, Elizabeth. This way we get the story and we save on hospital bills."

"You can write your own story," she said, clearly fighting to control her temper. "You know how Celine and I feel about each other. How can you even suggest that we work together?"

"I thought you were a professional," he said smoothly.

"I am, but—"

Tom patted her shoulder. "No, you're right," he said. "If you can't work with Celine, you can't. But in that case, do you think you could let me have your notes so she and I can go over them toge—"

The door slamming shut was all the answer he needed.

The room was dark. The figure lying on the bed was totally still, staring up at the pattern the light outside made on the ceiling. Except for the ticking of the bedside clock and the occasional muted sound of whimpering from the bed, the room was silent as well as dark.

Someone knocked gently on the door. "Are you all right?" a sweet female voice called. "I thought I heard a hamster in distress in there."

The figure on the bed didn't move.

The knocking came again. "I know someone's in there. I distinctly heard moaning."

"Go away!" he ordered.

The doorknob turned.

"Winston!" Denise snapped on the overhead light. "Winston, what are you doing? Are you all right?"

"I'm having a trauma," Winston said, slowly turning to face her. "Leave me alone."

Denise was in many ways one of the most perfect women Winston had ever known. She was intelligent, she was funny, she was practical and resilient, she didn't panic easily, she was full of common sense, and she was beautiful. She did, however, have one or two flaws. The most obvious one was that she never did what she was told.

"I will not leave you alone," she said, marching into the room. "You were going to help me study for my French midterm tonight, remember?"

"I can't," Winston groaned. "I'm too miserable."

Denise plopped down on the side of his bed. "Now what?" she asked. "Don't tell me you think you're losing your hair again."

"Hahaha, very funny," Winston snapped. "And anyway, Ms. Waters, if you had two grandfathers whose heads looked like Ping-Pong balls, you wouldn't think it was anything to laugh about."

She reached out for his hand. "I'm sorry, Winnie. I didn't mean to make fun of you. Tell Aunt Denise what's wrong."

Winston didn't need much coaxing. Not when it came to Denise. The only thing he was afraid to tell her was how madly in love he was with her. As close as they'd become since the beginning of school, she'd never given him any reason for thinking he would ever be more than a friend to her. A very good friend—a close, true, forever kind of friend—but just a friend. "My parents are coming on Friday," he told her gloomily.

Denise nodded. "Uh-huh . . ."

"You don't understand." Winston sat up. "My father is a man who had four brothers. He killed his first rabbit when he was six years old, Denise. He was an Eagle Scout. He joined the marines when he was eighteen. He walks up mountains in snowstorms for fun."

Denise was staring back at him uncomprehendingly. "So?"

"So you're not paying attention, Denise. My father's a man's man. He eats raw meat because he likes it. With raw egg on it, can you believe that? The chance of food poisoning is incredible. Plus, it's revolting."

She was trying not to laugh, but not trying hard enough, in Winston's opinion. "He wants to take you out to dinner on Parents' Weekend, is that the problem?"

Winston sighed. "No, that's not the problem," he snapped. "The problem is, he can't wait to meet my girlfriend."

Denise's eyebrows rose a fraction. She'd finally managed to stop laughing. "What girlfriend?"

He groaned. "Exactly. What girlfriend?"

"Winston Egbert!" she cried in mock-horror. "You didn't tell your parents you have a girlfriend, did you?"

"Sort of," he mumbled, praying she wouldn't start laughing again.

"Sort of? Winnie, why did you lie to them?

What does it matter whether you have a girlfriend?"

Winston tried to explain. "It matters to my father, Denise. He's never exactly considered me the son of his dreams." Winston sighed. "Of course, the son of his dreams would have been Rambo, but my dad doesn't see it that way. He thinks I'm a weakling. The one time he took me mountain climbing with him, I twisted my ankle getting out of the car and we had to go back home."

To her credit, Denise was still trying not to laugh, but she couldn't keep back a smile. "I still don't see what that has to do with you having a girlfriend."

"My father watches talk shows, Denise. He knows all about men who dress like women and men who dress like chickens and stuff like that."

She'd stopped laughing and was looking thoughtful. "Yes . . ."

"Well, when he found out I was living in a girls' dorm, he got all weird about it."

"Weirder than you did?" Denise asked with a smirk.

"Denise, please. I'm trying to be serious. He thought maybe I had, you know, tendencies . . . That that finally explained why I don't like to kill unarmed animals."

She cocked her head to one side. "Are we talking about homosexual tendencies?"

Winston nodded. "My father is. So that's

why I made up this girlfriend, you know . . ."

One of Denise's other flaws was that she had a habit of going right past the point he was making to another, totally different point.

"So what if you did have homosexual tendencies?" she demanded. "What's wrong with that?"

"Denise, the man eats raw ground beef. Will you give me a break, please? My father is not liberated, all right? He thinks that guys should date girls, not other guys."

"I don't see what the problem is," Denise said. "You don't date anybody."

"That's just the problem," Winston moaned. "I do. I date the most wonderful woman at SVU. I've told him all about her. What she looks like, what she's studying, what she likes, what she says . . ."

"What's her shoe size?"

"Seven and a half."

Denise shook her head. "Does this paragon have a name, too?"

Winston nodded.

She gave him a shove. "So what is it? Aphrodite?"

Winston studied the pattern on the bedspread for a few seconds. "Denise."

"Yeah?" she replied, as though he was about to ask her a question.

He kept his eyes on the bed. "No, that's her name. Denise."

She grabbed hold of the front of his shirt. She was really too strong for a woman, if you asked him.

"Denise what, Winnie?"

"Waters," he bleated. "Denise Waters."

Instead of letting go, she pulled harder, threatening to choke him.

"It just came out, Denise," he gasped. "I wasn't thinking, I—"

"So I guess you want me to pretend to be your girlfriend while your parents are here, is that it, Win?"

He could only stare at her in disbelief. It hadn't even entered his mind to suggest such a thing. He'd been planning to say that his girl-friend, the most perfect woman he'd ever known, was away for the weekend and see how his father took that.

"Would you?" Winston breathed.

"For a price."

"Anything," Winston babbled. "Anything at all."

She let go of his shirt. "You pay for the pool table for the next two years."

Jessica's long blond hair flew behind her as she marched toward the parking lot, her sister thundering behind her in hot pursuit.

"Don't think you can get out of this just by running away!" Elizabeth was shouting after her. "You're going to have to face up to things this time. This time you've really done it!"

If you only knew how well I've done it this time, Jessica thought, finally reaching the car. *If they gave prizes for screwups I'd win them all.*

She turned to her sister, her face showing nothing. "I'm not running away, Elizabeth," she said with exaggerated patience, even though she'd been more or less running since she came out of the coffeehouse to find Elizabeth waiting for her with that I-want-to-talk-to-you look in her eye. "I told you. It's my night to cook supper. I have to get home."

Elizabeth looked dumbfounded. "I don't believe you, Jess, I really don't. You move in with a man you hardly know and you don't tell anyone. What were you thinking? How did you think you could get away with it?"

"I wasn't trying to get away with anything. It just happened so fast." Jessica took out her keys. "You wouldn't understand, Elizabeth, because you never let anything just happen. You plan everything. I'm a woman of impulse."

"You're a woman in a whole lot of trouble," Elizabeth replied. She was shaking her head. "I just can't believe you didn't even tell *me*. I know we haven't been very close since school started, but I am your twin sister."

Jessica mentally crossed her fingers as she climbed into the Karmann Ghia. "I was going to tell you, Elizabeth," she promised. "I really was."

"Oh, yeah?" Jessica didn't have to look over to know that her sister's hands were on her hips. "When?"

"Soon."

"Well, now you don't have to tell me, because I know," Elizabeth said flatly. "But you can't just walk off now. We have to discuss this. We have to decide what you're going to tell Mom and Dad."

"Not now." How could Jessica decide what she was going to tell her parents when she wasn't planning to tell them anything? "Because as it happens, Elizabeth, I do have to cook dinner." She smiled serenely. "We're having pasta and seafood. Mike loves pasta and seafood."

"Jessica!" Elizabeth stepped back as Jessica slammed the door shut. "Look at me, will you? We have to talk about this. I'm worried about you, and so is Steven. We have to sit down and—"

Jessica rolled down the window. "This is why I didn't tell you," she said. "I knew you'd overreact, Elizabeth. You always overreact. You always make everything bigger than it is. If you're not careful you're going to ruin your skin with all that worrying."

"It's your skin I'm going to ruin," Elizabeth snapped back. "What are Mom and Dad going to say, Jess? Have you given any thought to that?"

Had she given any thought to it? She'd given it more thought than the UN gave to world peace.

"I don't think there's any reason to tell them just yet," Jessica answered coolly. She put the key in the ignition. "As long as I'm doing all right in school, what do they care where I live?"

They didn't call Elizabeth brainy for nothing. "But are you doing all right in school?" she wanted to know. "You have been going to classes and working, haven't you? Midterms are soon."

Who needed a mother when they had a sister like Elizabeth? Jessica leaned out the window. "Of course I know midterms are coming, Elizabeth. I'm living with Mike, not camping in the Himalayas. Isabella's going to study with me. I'll be fine."

But Elizabeth wouldn't give up.

"What about Saturday?" she demanded. "What happens when Mom and Dad meet Mike on Saturday? What are you going to tell them about him?" Elizabeth hesitated, searching for the right words. "He's not exactly a typical all-American college boy," she said at last. "Don't you think they're going to get suspicious?"

"They're not going to meet him on Saturday," Jessica said as the engine roared to life.

Elizabeth grabbed hold of the door. "What do you mean, they're not going to meet him?"

"Mike doesn't want to meet them." Jessica

threw the car into reverse, but she couldn't back up because her sister was still holding on to the window frame.

"Why not?" Elizabeth demanded. "Why doesn't he want to meet them?"

Jessica tossed her hair. "He just doesn't, that's all. Families aren't exactly his scene."

Elizabeth leaned in through the open window. "What is his scene, *exactly?*"

Jessica gunned the engine. "I really have to go now, Elizabeth. I'll see you before Mom and Dad get here so we can get our stories straight."

As she pulled out of the parking lot Jessica glanced into the rearview mirror. Elizabeth was standing in the space she'd just left, gazing after her.

Grace Harper was already sipping a cup of coffee when Nina arrived at the coffeehouse. Nina had expected her mother to be annoyed that she was late, but instead she greeted her with a big smile.

"Sit down, darling," she ordered. "I have some wonderful news."

The reason Nina was late was that she'd been walking around the quad in circles, rehearsing what she was going to tell her mother about her decision to stay at SVU.

"I have some news, too," Nina said.

Her mother patted her hand. "Let me tell

193

you mine first, sweetheart. You're going to be thrilled."

Grace Harper wasn't going to be thrilled at Nina's news, but Nina felt she had to tell her mother before she lost her nerve.

"This is pretty important," Nina began.

"When did you start being so impatient, Nina?" her mother wanted to know. "That's not like you at all." She rested her hands on the table. "Listen to me: it's all arranged. You'll take your midterms here, and then you'll be able to finish out the semester at home. Your grades are so far above average that your teachers have agreed to let you study on your own." She leaned back, smiling happily. "Isn't that wonderful?"

"No," Nina said, surprising herself with her bluntness. "It's not wonderful."

Grace Harper was still smiling, but the smile was slightly confused. "What did you say?"

"I said it's not wonderful," Nina repeated. She took a deep breath and rushed on. "I've decided not to leave SVU, Mom. I know I was really upset at first and all I could think of was getting away, but now I've decided to stay." She shredded the paper napkin in her hands. "You don't change things that are wrong by pretending they don't exist."

The smile vanished. "Who ever said anything about *changing* things?" Nina's mother asked.

"I want to make a difference," Nina said

firmly. "That's what I want. You and Dad have lived your lives the way you thought was best. Now it's my turn to live mine my way."

Grace Harper picked up the menu and began to study it. "You're still suffering from the aftereffects of shock, Nina, or you wouldn't be talking like this."

Now that she'd started, Nina was feeling more confident. She knew that if Bryan and Elizabeth were here, they'd be cheering her on.

"If I hadn't been suffering from the aftereffects of shock, I would have been talking like this a lot sooner," Nina argued. "It's taken me a while to figure out how I really feel, but now I'm sure. I've started a life for myself here, Mom, and I don't want to leave it. I definitely don't want to leave it to live the life you want for me."

The menu still in her hands, Mrs. Harper stared at her daughter in silence for several seconds. "And you don't think your father and I have any say in this?" she asked at last.

Nina shook her head slowly. "Not really," she answered softly. "After all, I have my scholarship. If you and Dad are too angry to speak to me—"

Her mother reached across the table and took her hand. "Nina," she said in her most reasonable voice. "You do understand that your father and I only want what's best for you, don't you?"

"You want what's best for you," Nina replied gently. "You want me to be like you two are, but

I'm not. I've only just started to learn that, but I know it's true. It's not that I don't love you and Dad; it's just that I'm not you. I'm me."

Grace Harper didn't say anything for what seemed like minutes. "You sound just like I did at your age," she said at last. "Your grandmother wanted me to stay at home and marry my high school sweetheart, but I was determined to go to college and have a career." She released Nina's hand. "And you're determined to change the world." She smiled wryly. "I take it you're not planning to change the world all by yourself. There's a certain young man you'd accept a little help from?"

"I'm really hungry all of a sudden," Nina said, hoping to change the subject. She ducked behind her menu so her mother couldn't see her blush.

It had been one of the worst days in memory for Elizabeth. First the discovery that Tom Watts was not only dating Celine but had decided to work with her on the story instead of herself, and then the frustrating scene with Jessica.

She was still reeling when she ran into Nina on her way to visit Bryan in the hospital and Nina invited her along.

"Why not?" Elizabeth said. "I'd like to be there when you tell Bryan you told your mother you're staying. I could use at least one happy ending in this miserable day."

Nina glanced worriedly at her as they left the campus. "What do you think you're going to do about Jessica?" she asked. "Are you going to tell your parents the truth?"

Elizabeth shrugged. "I don't know what to do," she admitted. "Half of me thinks they deserve to know, but the other half believes that it's Jessica's life and it's up to her to tell or not tell them." She kicked a small branch out of their path. "What I can't get over is *him*," she went on. "What a creep. He doesn't even want to meet our parents. He must be worried they'll take one look at him and realize what a loser he is." She hugged her books to her chest. "After all, my father is a lawyer. He could have Mike McAllery checked out if he wanted, and I'm sure he wouldn't find out anything good."

"What about Jessica?" Nina asked as they climbed the hospital stairs. "Do you think she'll tell them?"

Elizabeth laughed. Jessica had never voluntarily told the truth in her life. "Only if she has to."

"I guess the good news is that now that you're off the secret society story, you'll have more time to talk to Jessica and figure out what to do," Nina mused. "Maybe you'll even convince her to move back to the dorm."

Elizabeth held open the door. Her eyes were flashing. "Who said I'm off the secret society story?"

"You did," Nina answered, seeming a little

surprised by the edge in Elizabeth's voice. "You said Tom said—"

The golden hair swished as Elizabeth defiantly shook her head. "What Tom Watts says and what I do are not the same thing," she said shortly. "He may not want me to work with him, but he can't stop me from going ahead on my own."

Nina led the way to Bryan's ward. "That tone in your voice. It wouldn't be because you're upset that Tom's seeing Celine, would it?"

"It's nothing personal," Elizabeth said, trying to get whatever tone it was out of her voice. "The only person I'd like to see dating Celine is Mike McAllery. They deserve each other."

Nina stopped at the door to Bryan's room, prepared to knock, but the door was already ajar. She pushed it open. "I don't believe this!" she whispered.

Elizabeth looked over her shoulder. Grace Harper was sitting by the side of Bryan's bed. The two of them were laughing over something.

Bryan saw them first. "Hey, Nina!" he called. "Guess what? Your mom knew my dad in college."

"It's true," Grace Harper gasped. "I knew him well. He had so many crazy schemes, we used to call him Half Nelson."

Bryan and Mrs. Harper looked at each other and burst into another round of laughter.

"This really has been a strange day," Elizabeth whispered in Nina's ear.

Chapter Nine

Mike leaned over and gave her a kiss. "You go back to sleep," he whispered. "You deserve to spend the morning in bed."

Jessica kissed him back sleepily. "Don't you want me to get up and fix you some breakfast?"

His strong fingers stroked her sun-gold hair. "I think I can manage a cup of coffee and a bowl of cereal, baby. But if you want to be the perfect wife, you could bring me lunch later." He kissed her again. "If I have to work all weekend, a beautiful woman bringing me a picnic would make me a lot happier."

"One beautiful woman and one picnic will be delivered to your garage this afternoon," she promised, rolling over and pulling the covers over her head.

"Okay, Sleeping Beauty," Mike called as he left the room. "I'll see you later. Make sure you pack plenty of kisses in that basket."

Jessica lay still, listening to the clock tick and the sounds of Mike making himself breakfast. It didn't sound to her as though he was fixing a cup of coffee and a bowl of cereal. With the amount of time he was taking and all that noise, he couldn't be preparing less than a three-course meal. At last she heard the front door shut behind him. Jessica counted to three, in case he'd forgotten something, and then she leapt out of bed.

"I thought he'd never leave," she muttered as she grabbed her clothes and tore into the bathroom to take a quick shower. "If I don't get going, my parents will get to Isabella's before I do."

She was already out of the apartment before she remembered that she'd promised Mike she'd bring him lunch. How was she going to bring him a picnic when her parents would be expecting her to have lunch with them? She couldn't quite resist an impish smile as she raced down the stairs. It would almost be worth telling them the truth just to see their faces when she said, *Oh, I'm afraid I can't eat with you today. I promised my husband I'd bring him a picnic.*

Almost worth it, but not quite. Jessica jumped the last two steps and flew through the entrance.

"I'm sure I'll think of something," she told herself as she threw herself into her car. "I just wish I knew what."

Elizabeth had slept badly. Celine had done nothing but talk about Tom while she was getting ready for bed last night, and the result was that Elizabeth's dreams had featured Tom, Jessica, and Mike McAllery, all of them running away from her and laughing hysterically every time she got close.

Elizabeth picked up her hairbrush, her eyes on the sleeping Celine. Elizabeth usually found that the sight of someone sleeping made her feel more fondly toward them, even if she didn't feel that fondly toward them when they were awake. She didn't have this problem with Celine. Most people looked vulnerable and almost childlike when they were sleeping, but Celine looked just as poisonous and domineering as she did awake.

Celine suddenly smiled in her sleep. It was the smile she put on whenever a man came on the scene. Maybe Celine was dreaming about Tom.

Elizabeth winced as she brushed too hard through a tangle. *If that's the kind of girl Tom Watts wants to date, then he's welcome to her,* she told herself angrily, rubbing her head. *He's obviously not the man I thought he was at all.*

She put down the brush and stared at her reflection in the mirror. Appearances could certainly be deceptive. Except for little differences in hairstyle and makeup, she might be looking at her twin sister's face, and yet they were such different people it was a wonder they were related at all.

She glanced back at Celine. Celine had the face of an angel and the heart of a gunslinger. And Tom, too. Tom gave the impression of being straightforward and direct, and yet there were more secret corners and surprises to him than anyone she'd ever known.

And what about the head of the secret society? Elizabeth wondered. She had a pretty good idea of what he was like inside, but what was he like on the surface? She couldn't shake the feeling that she knew who it was; she just wasn't allowing herself to see him clearly. She was convinced that Tom was right, it wasn't Peter Wilbourne. But she'd spent so long believing that it was, it was hard to change her thinking and erase Peter's face from her picture of the man. *Someone less involved in campus politics,* she told herself. *Someone who has money . . . someone no one knows much about . . . someone who is smart and charismatic and comes and goes as he pleases . . .*

She continued to stare at the mirror, almost able to see a face in front of hers, a pale, ghost-like face that belonged to the man she was seeking. But just as it seemed as if it might take on substance, it vanished.

"I see you're all ready to spend the day with your parents," Celine drawled. "Don't you look adorable."

Although it was tempting, Elizabeth decided

not to start the day by exchanging insults with Celine. She was going to need all her strength to deal with Jessica today. "What about your parents?" she asked pleasantly. "What time are they arriving?"

Celine yawned. "My parents? Are you kidding? My parents wouldn't be caught dead at something like this. How corny can you get?"

Elizabeth gave her roommate one of her sweetest smiles. Maybe she could risk one little insult. "What a shame," she said. "I was looking forward to meeting them. I bet Nina a dollar that they actually are human."

Jessica leaned forward in the passenger seat of the Jeep, as though trying to push it along. "Can't you go any faster, Elizabeth?" she demanded. "What if Mom and Dad arrive at my dorm before we do?"

Elizabeth didn't take her eyes from the road or press her foot down on the gas pedal.

"That's your problem, Jess, not mine," she informed her sister. "I said I'd keep quiet today and give you a chance to decide how you want to handle things, but that's all. I'm not getting a ticket for speeding just because you couldn't be torn away from your boyfriend long enough to spend one night in your own bed."

Jessica looked over at her. "Did you used to be this catty?" she asked. "Or is this part of your personality change since we came to college?"

"Don't worry about my personality change," answered Elizabeth, slowing down at the intersection. "Worry about yours." She turned left.

"What are you doing?" Jessica swung around in her seat. "You turned left. You're not supposed to turn left here; you're supposed to turn right."

Elizabeth gave her a disinterested glance. "I thought we'd go to that bakery on Buena Vista and get some stuff for breakfast."

"You're doing this deliberately, aren't you?" Jessica demanded. "You're just trying to force the issue?"

It was typical of Elizabeth to try to ruin everything. Everyone had always thought Jessica was the troublemaker, but she herself was sure that Elizabeth and her principles had caused a lot more trouble over the years than her own little white lies and fibs had.

"Don't be ridiculous, Jess," Elizabeth said. "I'm doing this to make everything seem relaxed and normal. Mom and Dad will think it's very grown up of us to have thought of having something ready for them to eat after the drive."

"I bet," Jessica grumbled. "Just don't think this little scheme of yours is going to work, Elizabeth, because it won't. Even if we're not there, Isabella will be, and she'll cover for me."

Elizabeth stopped the Jeep outside the tiny bakery. Jessica had left the apartment so quickly this morning that she hadn't had time for so much as a glass of juice. Her stomach growled as the fragrant aromas of fresh bread and pastries drifted toward the car.

"Good," Elizabeth said, opening the door. "Then we'll have plenty of time to pick up some coffee and fruit, too."

Mrs. Wakefield looked into the bedroom. "Well, I see being a college girl hasn't made you any neater," she said to Jessica. "I don't have to ask which side of the room is yours. It's the one that looks like a hurricane hit it."

Jessica laughed. "I don't have time to spend on housework," she told her mother. "I have a lot of studying to do, you know."

Mr. Wakefield winked at Elizabeth and Isabella. "We all know what Jessica's studying, don't we?" he joked. "Advanced Boys, and Shopping 12.8."

"Jessica doesn't have to take those courses," Mrs. Wakefield said, turning back from the bedroom. "She could teach them."

Elizabeth risked a glance at Isabella, who at that same moment was risking a glance at her. For the first time it occurred to Elizabeth that Isabella Ricci might turn out to be an ally. It was obvious from the way she'd made the apartment look as though Jessica still lived there that she cared a lot about her; it was also obvious from the way she was looking at Elizabeth that she was as worried about Jessica as she was.

Mr. Wakefield put an arm around Elizabeth. "Now where?" he asked. "You girls going to show us around the campus? Introduce us to all your new friends?"

Both Elizabeth and Isabella looked to Jessica.

Jessica smiled back as though she'd made a million new friends since the beginning of the semester and couldn't wait for them all to meet her parents.

"Now there's a good idea," she said brightly. "Should we walk or take the Jeep?"

Celine couldn't seem to stop talking.

"I can't tell you how I've been looking forward to meeting Elizabeth's parents," she was saying for at least the third time. She smiled so hard at Mr. Wakefield that Elizabeth was worried he might wither. "You must be very proud of her," she gushed. "She's so smart and so *interested* in things." The honey-colored eyelashes fluttered. "Not like me. I'm just very ordinary."

"Yeah, just your ordinary, run-of-the-mill shark," Jessica whispered.

Mr. Wakefield continued to smile mushily back at her, slightly mesmerized by the buckets of Southern charm Celine was pouring on, but the Boudreaux charm didn't have the same effect on Mrs. Wakefield.

"It's been very nice meeting you, too, dear,"

she said, holding out her hand. "But I'm afraid we're going to have to leave now. There's so much to see."

Celine was immediately apologetic. "Oh, of course you do," she said in a rush. She turned to Elizabeth. "Have they met the devastatingly handsome William yet?" she asked. "I bet that's where you're rushing off to. Lunch with William."

Jessica groaned quietly, but Elizabeth didn't look over. She was too busy watching the look her parents exchanged at the mention of William. Somehow, although she'd told them in letters that she and Todd were no longer a couple, she hadn't managed to mention William.

Celine galloped on. "Not only is your daughter one of the brainiest women at SVU," she said, "but her boyfriend is probably the most sophisticated man on campus."

Mr. Wakefield's smile became suddenly solid. Obviously he didn't think sophisticated was necessarily a positive quality.

Elizabeth glanced at her sister. It was clear that they were both thinking the same thing. If Mr. Wakefield was going to think William White was too sophisticated for his daughter, what was he going to think of Mike McAllery?

"Is that so?" Mrs. Wakefield asked. She looked at Elizabeth. "I can't wait to meet this young man."

"Me neither," Elizabeth said.

*   *   *

"It certainly is a shame about Jessica spilling that grape juice all over her, isn't it?" Mr. Wakefield said, cutting another piece from his chicken.

"Um," Elizabeth said. She had watched with grudging admiration as Jessica tipped the entire pitcher over herself.

"Though I don't see why she couldn't join us for lunch after she changed," Mr. Wakefield went on. "I know she has a lot to do all week and needs Saturday for errands, but it's not as though we come here every weekend."

Thank goodness, Elizabeth thought. She didn't know about Jessica, but her nerves couldn't stand it. So far her parents hadn't asked her anything about Todd or about William, but she could tell from the way her mother was admiring everything from the way the grounds were kept to the lunch menu that it wouldn't be long before they did. In the past few weeks at SVU, Elizabeth had stopped thinking of herself as her parents' little girl, but she could tell by her mother's glances that her parents hadn't.

"Now, there's a young man who's very sure of himself," Mrs. Wakefield said suddenly.

Elizabeth looked up. Her mother was gazing over her head at the entrance to the cafeteria. Expecting to see Peter Wilbourne and a gaggle of Sigmas, Elizabeth turned.

William White, elegant in his black linen suit

and an ivory silk shirt, stood in the doorway smiling with all the dazzle and remoteness of the sun. Instead of being happy to see him, as she knew she should be, Elizabeth was annoyed. She was never completely relaxed with William, and though her ill ease might escape her parents' attention tonight at a noisy, crowded dance, now they were bound to notice. Elizabeth sighed to herself. Who was she trying to fool? she wondered. Her parents or herself?

"Who's he waving at?" Mr. Wakefield asked through a mouthful of chicken. "He's not waving at us, is he?"

"I think he must be waving at Elizabeth," Alice Wakefield said. She leaned across the table to Elizabeth. "Celine didn't mention how very attractive he is," she said. "I take it that *is* the most sophisticated young man on campus."

Elizabeth nodded, watching William striding toward them.

"Whatever happened to Todd?" Mr. Wakefield asked. "I always liked him."

Mike leaned back against the wall of the garage with a satisfied sigh. "That was the best picnic I've ever had in my life," he murmured, slipping his arm around Jessica's waist. "There's just one teeny little thing it needs to make it perfect."

Jessica leaned against him dreamily. She was exhausted from rushing to meet her parents this morning and rushing back to bring Mike his lunch this afternoon. Being in one place when you were supposed to be in another was extremely stressful. Yet even though it was raining and they were sitting in a dirty garage, it had been the best picnic she'd ever had, too. "What teeny little thing?" she asked softly.

He pulled her close. "Dessert," he said, his lips against hers. "Remember the first time you came for dinner? Dessert's always been our favorite part of the meal, hasn't it?"

She could feel herself melting against him, all her resolve to get back to her family melting, too. "Not here," she whispered, not exactly pushing him away. "What if somebody comes?"

"You're my wife," he said, nuzzling her neck. "I'll make love to my wife wherever I want."

Jessica laughed. "Mike, I really think you're crazy."

"Come on, baby," Mike urged. "I'll lock up the garage and we can go in the back of the Buick." He touched her as though she were made of the most delicate glass. "Please, Jess."

She forced herself to glance behind him at the old kitchen clock on the wall. It was already three o'clock. Her parents were expecting her to meet them in front of the library at three thirty to finish looking around and attend the assembly for freshmen and their parents at five. If she didn't show up, Elizabeth might be forced to tell them where she was.

She kissed his eyelids and his smooth, dark brows. "I've got a better idea," she said, fighting off her desire to stay in Mike's arms. "Why don't we wait until tonight? That way we can start dinner with dessert."

"Why don't we have dessert twice?" Mike asked.

Elizabeth was standing between her parents at the entrance to the library, peering into the distance for a glimpse of a familiar golden head. Where was Jessica? Why did she always pick the worst times to go AWOL?

Mr. Wakefield checked his watch again. "We did tell Jessica three thirty, didn't we?"

"Yes, Ned," Alice Wakefield said. "We did tell her three thirty."

He jammed his hands in his pockets. "Where did she say she had to go?"

"She had some things to pick up in town," Alice Wakefield said patiently. She looked over at Elizabeth. "Isn't that right, Elizabeth?"

Elizabeth could tell from her mother's voice that she was getting suspicious. Avoiding actual eye contact, she nodded. "Maybe she ran into someone and started talking," Elizabeth suggested. "You know what Jess is like."

"Um . . ." Mrs. Wakefield said. "We know."

"Some boy, probably," said Mr. Wakefield.

"I imagine she has a lot of boyfriends."

Elizabeth laughed. "That's Jess."

"Same old Jess," her mother said. "I just hope she isn't spending all her time dating. I hope she's spending enough time at home, keeping up with her schoolwork."

"Oh, she is," Elizabeth said quickly, glad to have something that was almost the truth to say. "She's spending most of her time at home. I know that for a fact."

"Maybe that's where she is now," Mr. Wakefield said. "Talking on the phone."

This time it was Alice Wakefield who checked her watch. "The assembly's in fifteen minutes," she said. "Maybe you should go see if Jess is at her dorm, Ned."

Elizabeth's heart sank. What if they went to Jessica's dorm and ran into someone who knew that she didn't live there anymore? What if, on the way to Jessica's dorm, he passed Jessica herself in her bright red Karmann Ghia, racing to meet them?

"I've got a better idea!" Elizabeth cried, made reckless by desperation. "Why don't I show you the television station where I work? It's right over there." She had planned to keep them away from WSVU because of her most recent argument with Tom, but she would have to risk running into him in order to distract their attention from Jessica for a few minutes.

"I've never seen a television station first-hand," Ned Wakefield said.

"Well, now's your chance," said Elizabeth as she grabbed him by the arm and started across the quad.

Please don't be there, Tom, Elizabeth silently begged as she led her parents into the WSVU building. She showed them the recording studio. She showed them the editing room. She stopped at the door of the office itself. She couldn't hear anyone inside, but that didn't mean Tom wasn't there, hunched over his computer, getting his notes together for Celine.

"This is where the desks and computers are," she explained. "You know, where we actually write the stories."

"Do you have a desk in there?" Alice Wakefield asked. "Can we see?"

Before Elizabeth could think of some reason why her mother couldn't go into the office, someone else answered for her.

"Of course you can see the office."

The three Wakefields turned. Tom Watts had come up behind them, carrying a cardboard container of coffee. He extended his free hand. "I'm Tom Watts," he said, genuinely glad to see them. "You must be Elizabeth's parents. I've really been looking forward to meeting you." He gave them a lopsided and completely charming smile. "Elizabeth talks about you all the time."

"Does she?" Mrs. Wakefield said, with a glance at her daughter that said, *Well, she doesn't talk about you.*

"Come on." Tom opened the office door. "I'll show you around. You want a coffee or something? The machine's just down the hall."

"No, thanks," replied Mr. Wakefield. "We don't have much time."

"That's a shame," Tom said. "I was going to run one of the pieces Elizabeth and I worked on for you."

Elizabeth knew that though they hadn't said anything her parents hadn't liked William White. Alice Wakefield had smiled politely but coolly while William talked about himself, and Ned Wakefield had drummed his fingers softly on the tabletop, a sure sign that though he seemed to be paying attention, he was actually thinking of something else. But they liked Tom.

One minute Tom was introducing himself and the next the three of them were in the office, chatting away as though they'd known each other forever. Elizabeth stood in the hallway alone for a second, listening to their animated conversation, and then she followed them in.

"Will we see you and your parents later at the dance?" Mrs. Wakefield asked Tom when they were saying good-bye. "It would be lovely if you could join us."

It was as though Alice Wakefield had acci-

214

dentally said the magic word. Elizabeth watched the warmth evaporate from Tom's smile and his eyes become hard and empty.

"No," he said simply, beginning to shuffle restlessly. "No, that's very nice of you, but I'm afraid my—my parents couldn't make it this year."

Elizabeth could tell that he wanted to get away. It was always the same with Tom: just when you thought you were getting close, really getting to know him, he withdrew and put up an invisible shield around himself. What was the magic word? What was the secret he fought so hard to keep?

"What a shame," Mr. Wakefield said. "What about you, then? Why don't you come with us tonight? I'd love to talk more about the news program."

"I'm afraid I'm not a dancing man," Tom said, stepping backward into the office.

No, Elizabeth thought. *You're not a dancing man. You're a mystery man.*

This is a dream, Jessica was telling herself as her father's car left the SVU grounds. *A really, really bad dream. But I'm going to wake up from it. I'm going to wake up, and it will be Sunday morning and my parents will be back in Sweet Valley, and Mike will be beside me, and we'll have pancakes for breakfast.*

Jessica fought back the impulse to burst into

215

tears. This wasn't a dream. This was real. She was really being forced to go to dinner with her family even though she'd told them she had a date. "Never mind your date," her father had commanded. "You kept us waiting long enough, young lady. You'll spend the evening with us."

The tears were winning the battle. Jessica surreptitiously wiped her eyes with the sleeve of her jacket. What was she going to tell Mike? What was he going to say when she didn't come home in time for dinner? What was she going to say when he asked her where she'd been?

She looked over at Elizabeth, sitting beside her talking to their mother about some story she was working on. Jessica was grateful that Elizabeth had covered for her when she was late getting back for the assembly, but she couldn't help thinking that her twin could have backed her up a little more when she tried to get out of going for dinner. "Oh, come on, Jess," Elizabeth had hissed. "You can spare a couple of hours."

"What about you, Jessica?" Mrs. Wakefield asked. "Do you know anything about this secret society?"

At the sound of her name, Jessica wrenched her mind away from the fact that her entire life was being ruined in such a short time.

"Secret society?" She shrugged. "Someone told me that it's all just rumor. That probably one of the fraternities started it, just to wind everyone up."

Elizabeth shot her a look. She obviously thought that the someone Jessica was talking about was Mike, and she was going to hold that against him, too.

Much to Jessica's amazement, however, Elizabeth didn't argue with her. Instead she started asking Mrs. Wakefield questions about home.

Jessica, uninterested in whose lawn had been relaid on Calico Drive and what new shop had opened on Main Street, turned her attention back to the road. She let out a strangled cry. "Where are we going?" she demanded. "This isn't the way to the restaurant."

Her father turned the car right. "Of course it isn't. We're going to pick up Steven and Billie."

"Steven and Billie?" Not only wasn't this a dream, it wasn't even a nightmare. It was hell. She'd gone to hell. "But why can't they just meet us there?"

Alice Wakefield turned in her seat and looked at her closely. "Now what's wrong with you, Jessica? Surely you don't object to giving your brother a ride."

"Well, no, I—" What could she say? *We can't go to Steven's building because that's where I live and my husband will go wild if he sees us?*

Jessica looked at Elizabeth, but Elizabeth was staring out the window so intensely you'd think she'd never seen a California street before.

Maybe if she could wait in the car. She could tell them she had cramps and didn't feel like climbing all those stairs. They might believe that. Then she could just lie on the floor of the car till they came back.

To Jessica's enormous relief, Steven and Billie were standing in the parking lot waiting for them and Mike's Corvette was nowhere to be seen. *He's later than he said he'd be,* Jessica thought. *This part's going to be all right. We're not going to run into Mike.*

"You two climb in the back with the girls," Mr. Wakefield said. "We've got reservations for seven, so we better get a move on."

"That's right," Jessica chimed in. "We don't want to be late."

Steven smirked as he squeezed in beside her. "Since when are you so worried about being late?" he asked.

Suddenly her own mother destroyed her moment of peace. She asked to use Steven's toilet.

"Can't you wait till we get to the restaurant?" Jessica squealed.

"Jess is right," Mr. Wakefield said. "It won't take us much longer to get there than it'll take you to get upstairs and unlock the door."

The car started forward.

Jessica crossed her fingers, hard.

Mr. Wakefield stopped at the parking lot exit.

"Left or right, Steven?" he asked. "I always get confused coming out of here."

"Left," Steven said.

"Right," Billie said.

"I thought we were going to that Mexican place on Palm Drive," Elizabeth said. "Doesn't that mean we should go right?"

"It's shorter if you go left," Steven said.

"But easier to miss the turn," Billie said. "And there's that one-way part of San Sebastian to watch out for, too."

"You're the only one who ever gets caught up in the one-way," Steven said.

"And you're the one who always gets lost," Billie said.

Jessica didn't even see him drive up. All of a sudden, directly in front of them, waiting for a space in the traffic to turn left into the parking lot, was a customized '64 Corvette. In the passenger seat was the biggest bouquet of flowers Jessica had ever seen. In the driver's seat was Mike McAllery. She could feel Elizabeth glance over at her, but she couldn't move or speak.

"Go left," Mrs. Wakefield said.

"Go right," Elizabeth said.

Go somewhere! Jessica wanted to scream.

Mr. Wakefield decided to go left. He put on his signal and waited for the Corvette to make its turn. The driver looked over at them.

Frozen in horror, Jessica couldn't take her eyes from his.

Jessica opened the front door an eighth of an inch at a time, every cell of her body listening. There was nothing to hear. "Mike?" she called. "Mike?" She stopped, puzzled. The apartment smelled like a florist's. She looked down. A trail of flowers, most of them torn or crushed, led from the hallway into the living room.

"Mike?" she called, following the damaged petals. "Mike, I'm sorry. I'm so, so sorry. Can we please talk?"

He was sitting in the leather lounge chair, his back to her, his face to the closed blinds of the front window. The room was dark. "You're sorry?"

She took a step forward for each heavy beat of her heart. One. Two. Three.

"Yes, I am. I'm so sorry, Mike. I never meant . . ."

The chair swiveled around. "What did you mean, Jessica?" His voice was as calm and hard as a stone. "Did you mean to humiliate me, Jessica, is that what you meant? Did you mean to treat me like some stupid little boy? Did you mean to make a fool out of my feelings for you? Is that what you meant, Jess? Or was there something else? Some subtle little thing I've overlooked."

Jessica almost wished he'd start screaming. She wished she could see his face, look into his eyes. "Mike, I can explain. I really can." She'd thought about it all through dinner and all the way back here, and she knew that the only thing she could do was tell him the truth. Then they'd go to the dance together and she'd introduce him to her parents. *This is my husband,* she'd say. *This is the man I love.*

"So go ahead," Mike ordered. "Explain."

She reached for the light switch.

"Don't touch that!"

She jumped back as though he'd thrown something at her. "I just—I wanted to see you. We can't talk in the dark."

"Why not?" he shouted. "I've been living in the dark for weeks now. You've been keeping me there. You tell me one thing and then you do something else."

"But I didn't mean it!" Jessica wailed. "It's just that I couldn't tell my parents about us. I don't know why; I just couldn't."

"I know why!" He kicked the chair back as he stood up. "Because you didn't want to tell them, Jess. You're ashamed of me. You with your nice cozy, middle-class family; what would they think about me, huh? Your brother hasn't been shy about hiding his opinion of me, and your sister's no better. I saw the way she was looking at me in the car, Jess. She thinks I'm the scum of the earth."

"But I don't care what she thinks," Jessica sobbed.

He started coming toward her. "Yes, you do." He kicked the coffee table out of his way. He knocked over a lamp. "You care, Jessica. You care or you wouldn't have lied to me the way you have. You wouldn't have lied to your family."

Jessica started walking backward. "Mike, please," she moaned. "If we can just sit down and—" She bumped into the wall.

"It's too late," he said, grabbing her by the shoulders. "We've gone past talking, Jessica. Way past. We passed talking at about ninety miles an hour."

"Mike! Please!" Though Jessica's own eyes were filled with tears, she could now see his face by the foyer light. It was ravaged with crying, the golden eyes swollen and rimmed with red, his skin drained of color.

"I want to hit you," he said. "I've never wanted to hit anybody so much in my life." His grip tightened on her shoulders. "I want you to hurt the way you're hurting me, Jessica. That's what I want. I want you to feel the hurt the way I am. I want you to beg me for mercy."

She was too terrified to scream. "Mike . . ." Her eyes were streaming, her body was shaking uncontrollably. "Mike, please . . ."

All of a sudden he shoved her hard and she

fell to the ground. "Get away from me!" he screamed. "Get away!"

"Mike!"

"What are you, deaf? Lock yourself in the bathroom, Jessica! Get away from me before I do something I'll really regret!"

"In spite of Jessica's incredible behavior, I'm really glad your father and I came up today," Mrs. Wakefield was saying.

"I'm glad you did, too," Elizabeth said, even though there were so many thoughts racing around in her head that she was only giving her mother half her attention.

Mrs. Wakefield sighed the way, as the mother of Jessica Wakefield, she had sighed thousands of times in the past. "I suppose we should be happy that Jessica's adjusted so well to college life. She's so headstrong I did wonder what all the freedom would do to her. Not that I approve of her rushing off like that right after dinner, but at least we don't have to worry that she hasn't settled in or made any new friends."

Elizabeth gazed at the dance floor, where Steven and Billie were doing the twist and Todd and Enid kept darting looks at her. All the things going on at this dance would have been significant for her if her mind hadn't been totally taken up by Michael McAllery.

"Oh, she's settled in, all right," Elizabeth

said. "And she's definitely made new friends."

Michael McAllery. What was with him? Next to Michael McAllery, Tom Watts wasn't a man of mystery, Elizabeth decided, he was an open book.

Michael McAllery had some vague connection with the campus that no one could define but that kept him very much around. He was a womanizer who for some reason had decided to break all his own rules and live with Jessica. He was sure of himself. He was dangerous. He was hated by a lot of people, not the least of which was William White. The look on his face when the Corvette screeched past them earlier came into her mind. He had a bad temper, too.

"Elizabeth, Elizabeth, are you listening to me?" Mrs. Wakefield reached across the table.

Elizabeth focused on her mother. "I'm sorry," she said. "I guess I got distracted by the dancing."

"It's just that I wanted to talk to you, honey, while we have a few minutes to ourselves." She patted her hand. "I have to admit that I was worried about you when you first arrived. Your letters sounded so down and so unlike you . . ."

Elizabeth smiled. "I'm fine, Mom, really. I'm doing well in my classes, and I've got Nina, and William . . ."

"And Tom," Alice Wakefield finished for her. "As soon as we met Tom I knew you were all right. Isn't that strange?" She looked toward the refreshment table, where William and Mr. Wakefield were lined up for punch. "Although I must say, I am a little concerned about this secret society story of yours. I know Jessica didn't seem to think there was anything in it—"

"Jessica doesn't know anything about it," Elizabeth cut in. *She believes anything Mike McAllery tells her,* she added to herself.

And suddenly her mind was back to Mike again. Why would he tell Jessica that the society didn't exist? Why had he lied? Since he had never actually attended the college, he'd been at SVU longer than your average student, which meant that, unlike William, he'd been here long enough to have seen for himself that the rumors were true. *He lied because he wanted Jessica to tell me I was wrong,* Elizabeth answered herself.

Elizabeth's mother started talking about the last dance she'd attended at SVU. Her father and William were walking slowly toward them, carefully carrying paper cups.

"That really was in the sixties," Mrs. Wakefield was saying. She smiled at the memory. "Can you imagine? I wore this short pink dress that must have made me look like a cocktail frank."

But Elizabeth didn't hear her; there was too much commotion going on in her head. Words were crashing together, like the pieces of some gigantic puzzle falling into place. *The last person you'd ever suspect . . . no ties to the Sigmas . . . no*

225

*real ties to the college . . . smart, really smart . . . a
manipulator . . . someone who works alone . . . someone dangerous . . . someone sure of himself . . . someone with a temper . . .*

Michael McAllery! The leader of the secret
society was Michael McAllery! It had to be.
Wait till she told Tom.

Elizabeth jumped to her feet. "I've got to
go, Mom," she announced. "I won't be long,
but I've got to go."

Mrs. Wakefield opened her mouth but was
clearly too surprised to make any protest.

Elizabeth rushed on. "I just remembered
something. Something important that I forgot
to do." She held up her hands. "Twenty minutes, Mom. Tell Dad and William I'll be back in
twenty minutes."

"What is it with you girls all of a sudden?"
her mother called after her. "You can hardly sit
still for more than ten minutes."

"Come on, Tombo," Danny was urging him.
"You can miss one night of work to go to the
movies. Isabella says it's a great double feature."

Tom didn't turn from the computer. "I
can't, Danny. I really can't. I've got too much
to do."

"But it's Saturday night, man. Isabella and I
figured we'd go for avocado pizza after the
flicks."

Tom kept typing and didn't say anything. He knew Danny well enough to know that if he kept answering him, they'd keep arguing, but if he didn't speak, Danny would soon give up.

"Isabella has got that new Brothers in Blues CD you like. We could listen to it on the way."

Tom typed another sentence.

"We really wish you'd come with us, Tom. How much work are you going to get done anyway with that racket coming from the dance at Xavier Hall? Why don't you relax a little? You've been even tenser than usual all day."

"I'll see you later, Danny."

Danny cleared his throat. "Tom—"

"Try not to wake me up when you get in."

Tom's fingers moved across the keyboard while his ears listened to the sound of Danny walking down the hallway. As soon as he heard the outside door bang closed, Tom ended his session on the computer and left the building by the other exit.

The lights of Xavier Hall burned brightly. Music and laughter poured into the night from every door and window, and across the front of the building a giant banner proclaimed WEL-COME, PARENTS.

Tom tried not to look or listen as he walked past, but the waving sign seemed to be calling to him, "Welcome, Parents! Welcome, Parents!"

Tom jammed his hands into his pockets and

hurried on. There were some parents who could never be welcomed anywhere ever again. Parents who would never dance or laugh or sing, never see their sons grow up.

The party sounds followed him across the campus and to his dorm. Once inside his room Tom locked the door, lighting a candle instead of turning on the light.

Until recently, the metal chest had stayed hidden and untouched at the back of his closet for months. Now he took it down for the second time, carefully laying out its few contents on his desk. The world that contained welcoming banners and loud music moved as far from Tom as the sun as he sat at his desk, staring at the tiny china rabbit while he fingered the silver football on the charm bracelet.

The knock on the door was so unexpected that he jumped.

"Tom? Tom, are you in there?" It was Elizabeth's voice, breathless and urgent. "Tom, if you're in there, I really have to talk to you. It's important."

Tom let go of the bracelet, his hand reaching for the ring shaped like a broken star.

She knocked again. "Tom, are you there? It's about the—you know, about the story. I think I've discovered something."

Tom's hand folded around the ring. *There's not much you can tell me that I don't already know,* he said silently.

She knocked one last time. He didn't turn around.

Elizabeth had hoped to bring Tom with her to Jessica's. She wasn't overjoyed at the prospect of facing Michael McAllery by herself. It would have been bad enough before, when he was just someone she disliked intensely, someone with a hold over her sister Elizabeth couldn't understand. Now that she was sure he was the head of the secret society, however, she was even more reluctant to confront him alone. He knew she was investigating the society; he might even be able to sense her suspicions about him.

"Tom's probably out on a date with Celine," she told herself angrily as she climbed into the Jeep. She threw the gearshift into first. "Well, I don't need his help. Let him fool around with the Southern Pill if he wants. I'll solve this story on my own."

Despite her brave words, all the while she was driving to Jessica's, Elizabeth practiced what she would say if Mike was at home. It was one way of ignoring the heavy hammering of her heart. *I'll make up some excuse for stopping by,* she told herself. Maybe she could say that Jessica had dropped an earring in the car earlier, or that Mrs. Wakefield had forgotten to give her something. Elizabeth turned into the parking lot of Jessica's building. *Then, when I'm leaving, I'll just ask Jess to walk me to the Jeep. What could be more normal than that?* Surely even someone as domineering as Mike McAllery couldn't object to that.

Elizabeth stopped by the mailboxes in the hallway, checking the apartment number: *McAllery 2A.*

"Here goes nothing," she whispered to herself as she slowly started to climb the stairs. What if Mike McAllery wouldn't let her in? What if he wouldn't let Jessica speak to her? What if—

Elizabeth stopped at the top of the stairs, staring at the door to 2A. What if the door was wide open and there was a trail of flowers leading inside?

"Jessica?" Elizabeth called, quietly stepping into the apartment. "Jessica?"

She hesitated at the entrance to the living room. It looked as though the apartment had been robbed and wantonly destroyed in the process. Furniture had been knocked over and things pulled off shelves and kicked into corners. And there were flowers everywhere.

"Jessica?" Elizabeth's feet crunched over the glass of a broken vase as she walked farther inside. "Jessica, it's me. Are you here?"

She held her breath, her body as rigid as concrete, waiting for Michael McAllery to come charging out of some corner, screaming and shouting and threatening her. Nothing happened.

"Jessica?" she called again, this time her voice a little louder. "Jess, where are you?"

"I'm in here," came the answer in a half-choked whisper. "Elizabeth?"

Jessica was sitting on the floor beside the bed, holding on to the spread like a drowning woman hanging on to a lifeline, her face and hair damp with tears.

Elizabeth rushed to take Jessica in her arms. "Jess, what happened? Who did this? Are you all right?"

Fresh tears streamed down her cheeks. "Mike," she whimpered. "We had this awful fight and he lost his temper and—" Her words were lost as sobs racked her body.

Elizabeth tightened her hold on her twin. "I'm taking you home," she told her calmly. "Do you hear me? Pack what you need tonight and I'll take you to Isabella's. I'll get Steven to come tomorrow for the rest of your things."

But Jessica was shaking her head. "I can't," she gasped. "I can't leave him. I just can't."

Elizabeth smoothed back damp strands of her sister's hair. "Yes, you can," she said, gentle but firm. "You just hold my hand and we walk out that door."

"No," sobbed Jessica. "You don't understand. I can't go."

"Why not?" Elizabeth demanded, trying not to let the rage she was feeling show in her voice.

"Has he threatened you, Jess, is that it? Are you so afraid of him? Is that why you can't leave?"

"No," Jessica whispered, wiping her eyes on the bedspread. "It's not that. It's nothing like that. It's—"

"What?" Elizabeth pressed. "What is it, Jess? What kind of hold does he have on you? Please tell me."

Jessica held her sister's eyes for a long moment before she held out her left hand.

"I married him."